EDNITA MANSION

Margaret Chirch

Inspiring Voices®
A Service of **Guideposts**

Inspiring Voices books may be ordered through booksellers or by contacting:

Inspiring Voices
1663 Liberty Drive
Bloomington, IN 47403
www.inspiringvoices.com
1 (866) 697-5313

Because of the dynamic nature of the Internet, any web addresses or
links contained in this book may have changed since publication and
may no longer be valid. The views expressed in this work are solely those
of the author and do not necessarily reflect the views of the publisher,
and the publisher hereby disclaims any responsibility for them.

Any people depicted in stock imagery provided by Thinkstock are
models, and such images are being used for illustrative purposes only.
Certain stock imagery © Thinkstock.

ISBN: 978-1-4624-0985-3 (sc)

Printed in the United States of America.

Inspiring Voices rev. date: 06/23/2014

CAST OF CHARACTERS

Edward T. Newburg
son of John and Caroline Newburg,

Mary Ellen,
Daughter of James and Pearl Cauldwell, also she is
Edwards's girlfriend, who was chosen by his parents

Juanita Sanchez
Orphan from Mexico
Also married to Edward

Margarita Sanchez,
mother to Juanita

Michael Dentin,
Edwards's friend

John and Elaine Pierson
Edwards's uncle and aunt (missionaries to China)

Grace Lynn Pierson
    daughter to John and Elaine Pierson and cousin to Edward

Gloria Grace Newburg and Maxwell Mitchell Newburg (Glory and Max)
    twins of Edward and Juanita

Thomas Jenkins,
    Edward's business partner

Maxwell Mitchell,
    Edwards close friend

Charley and Mollie Nielson
    sheep ranch owners in New Zealand
    also adoptive parents of Mary Ellen's baby

Doctor Thomas Westin
    Doctor for Mollie Nielson
    and brother-in-law to Margo Westin (aka Margarita Sanchez)

Starlita Westin
    daughter of Margarita Sanchez and Danny Westin

Danny Westin,
    deceased brother to Dr. Thomas Westin
    married to Margarita Sanchez and father to Starlita

Charles Wingate
    husband to Mary Ellen Wingate (Cauldwell)

Carl Downey
    Pastor of church

Dr. Hathaway,
    Dr. at hospital

Irene Kirk,
    hospital nurse

Frank Grandamere,
    Father of injured girl

PART ONE

CHAPTER ONE

(Edward Newburg)

Wʜᴇɴ Eᴅᴡᴀʀᴅ T. Newburg had finished university, his Father, John Newburg had, as a reward, offered to give him a trip to where ever he wanted to go. This reward was for finally finishing university without getting thrown out. Earlier, he had come so close to being thrown out of university due to his shenanigans.

His Father expected him to want to go to some place in Europe when he made this offer to his son, but Edward had surprised him by choosing Mexico. His Father tried to change his mind but couldn't so he finally gave him his trip. His boy was a smart kid and had breezed through university by hardly studying at all.

He was hoping Edward would begin to grow up now and would soon settle down and marry Mary Ellen Cauldwell. That would be the best business move for all of them. He may have to threaten his son to get him to comply with his wishes, but if that's the way it had to be, so be it. His son did like money when he didn't have to earn it, so his dad knew how to get him to comply with his wishes most of the time.

Edward, while on his Mexico trip, met a girl named Juanita Sanchez. She was without a doubt the prettiest girl he had ever seen and she was just wandering around looking lost. He watched her for a while and finally he approached her. When he asked if he could help her, she shied away from him as if she was afraid of him. She also looked hungry. He kept some distance between them and talked to her quietly. He told her he was hungry and was going to get something to eat and he thought that maybe she could tell him where the best place to eat was located. She could even join him so he wouldn't have to eat alone. She could even help him with ordering because his Spanish wasn't very good. He would be glad to buy her dinner for her help that is if she was ready to eat. He said he was a stranger to the area and didn't know the best places to eat. He told her he was going to have to go back to the United States soon. His vacation was almost over.

It took him a little while to realize she understood everything he said to her. He wasn't sure at first, that she was understanding him. Where had she learned English so well?

Juanita thought she saw her chance to maybe, just maybe, get to the US. She was sure glad she had taken advantage of all the classes to learn English that were offered at school. She shyly shook her head and followed him the rest of the time he was there. She was his little shadow. She told him her name when he asked her but when he asked her how old she was, she said she thought she was fifteen but she wasn't sure. She finally, after much quiet talking together, told him she had run away from an orphanage and didn't want to go back. From what she told him, he thought she had been bullied by an older girl to the point she was afraid to go to sleep at night. She told him that, as soon as she could, she ran away. She said she wanted to go to the United States because she thought her mother, Margarita Sanchez went there when she left her at the orphanage.

CHAPTER TWO

H E HAD NO trouble getting her back to the United States for he was a very resourceful man and knew how to use his father's name. Edward told her he loved her and wanted to marry her but they would have to keep it a secret from his Father. Juanita, having grown up in an orphanage, had no point of reference about family or Fathers so she readily agreed. He bought her a little cheap ring and told her it would be the same as a big wedding if they said "I love you" to each other and he put a ring on her finger. He thought maybe he really did love this girl he had known for such a short time. He was sure he loved her more than he loved Mary Ellen Cauldwell that his father thought he should marry. He wished he could get her a nice ring, but the fact was, he was running out of money and his father was still after him to propose to Mary Ellen.

When his father pressed him, he told his father that rings cost money and he couldn't give Mary Ellen a cheap ring and that is all he could afford right now. His Father took the bait and told him by Monday morning there would be enough money in Edwards' account to buy any kind of ring he wanted. His father said he should take Mary Ellen out to dinner or where ever he wanted to go to propose to her.

Now, Edward thought, he would have enough money to do what he wanted for Juanita and still get a ring for Mary Ellen. Juanita did not doubt him about the marriage. She took what he said as truth. They had been staying in a cheap motel and he had to make other arrangements soon.

Edward and his friend Mitchell Dentin had bought a piece of land way out in the sticks of Indiana that had a shack on it. There was a pretty lake on it and he and Mitch and some of their friends had stocked the lake with fish and used to camp out there sometime. They had fixed the shack up some but he hadn't been there in a long time. The best thing about it was that his Father knew nothing about it. He could take Juanita there. He was glad he and his buddies had put in electricity. They had done that one day when there was a big game coming up and they would be at the "shack" and didn't want to miss the game. He had spent almost all of his money at the time getting electricity brought to the house from the main road. He would bring Juanita there and she could make it into a home for them.

He had earlier bought his friend's part in it when his friend needed money. He was so glad it belonged only to him.

CHAPTER THREE

AFTER HE HAD first taken Juanita out to the shack, he hated to leave her. He stayed with her a little while and talked to her telling her, in a couple of weeks he would have to be gone on a business trip and might be gone for quite a while but he would leave her plenty of supplies and would check in on her as often as he could.

Now that he had the money, he would put in a telephone for her. It would be costly to bring the line down to their house but he would do it. It took a few days to get it done but he had some pull with a name such as his. He went to see Juanita the day it was to be put in. She was so happy to see him and was overjoyed to think he was doing this for her. He also bought her a camera that she could take pictures with and it would develop them too. He wanted her to have a hobby so she wouldn't get too lonely when he had to be gone for long periods of time.

He asked her if she wanted anything else that he could get for her. She shyly said that she had learned to knit at the orphanage and would love to have some yarn and knitting needles. He knew nothing about this but he was sure going to find out.

He went to a mall and looked for what he thought was a store that sold these things. He went in and told the clerk he wanted knitting needles. She asked him what size he wanted. He thought a minute and said give me one of each. She looked at him and said just one of each? He said well do you think my girlfriend will need more than one? The lady said to him, Sir I think your girlfriend would like to have a pair of each size. He said ok. Then he told her, "I really just don't know anything about it but I wanted to surprise her with this". She laughed and said I think she would be surprised with only one needle of each size. She then began to give him a little lesson on how to knit. They laughed together and he told her to fix up a nice package of everything she might need.

When Edward brought the knitting supplies to Juanita, she was amazed at all the things that he had purchased. He also bought her a radio. He had drawn up some plans to renovate the house. He showed her what he had planned. She marveled at the room she would have when it was finished. When he asked if there was any other thing she would want built while he had the builders out there. She told him she would love to have a porch across the front. He added that to the plans. When she asked what is this pointing to one section of the plans? He told her it was a bathroom. She said "inside?" and he assured her it was. She sat there and just stared at him and all at once she jumped up and made a big leap and landed in his lap, with her arms around his neck.

This surprised and pleased him so because this was the first time she had been that demonstrative with him.

Edward was friends with the man in charge of the renovation of the house. He cautioned him that he should make sure his men were all trustworthy and would treat his wife with respect. His friend said he would do that and Edward would have nothing to worry about. Edward told Juanita he would be gone for about one month, but he would call her on the telephone very often, and would get back as soon as possible. He explained to her if the telephone rings, she should pick up the phone and say nothing until she heard his voice. Then they could talk. For the next two days he tried the telephone until he was sure she understood. He knew he had to get busy on his proposal to Mary Ellen.

CHAPTER FOUR

WHEN EDWARD WENT to get the ring for Mary Ellen, he had spent so much money already but he wanted to get something showy. He went to a pawn shop and looked at the rings there. He had a buddy from university who told Edward about his uncle's pawn shop and said he would give him a good deal. He found the ring he wanted. It was a beautiful ring and it looked as good as any he had looked at in the jewelry stores.

When he took Mary Ellen out for dinner and proposed to her he had such mixed feelings he just almost didn't do it. He felt she was such high society that she didn't care about him but just how high up the society ladder she could climb when they were married. It was all just a sham. She and her mother had been working on this wedding for months even though he hadn't even proposed to her yet but her answer, when he asked her about it was, well, we knew it was just a matter of time and it was also a matter of time in getting the place for the right venue that we wanted. We knew you had been busy, so we just went ahead with it.

He would be glad when it was over. He called Juanita every chance he could and she sounded so happy it made him want to cry. He wanted to be with her and enjoy seeing her happiness when she discovered something new. He knew that the sooner he got the wedding over with, the quicker he could see Juanita again.

He started rushing the plans, saying he couldn't wait to be married. They set the date up sooner and he said he had plans for the honeymoon already made. So they hurried the wedding along.

He had made arrangements for them to go to a plush hotel in Canada that one of his friends had told him about. It had pretty scenery and he knew Mary Ellen would like it because it had many amenities. As soon as the wedding and reception was over, the bride and groom left for Canada. He told Mary Ellen he could only get the hotel for two weeks because they were so booked but she didn't seem to mind. She said she was excited to get home and start their life together as husband and wife.

Her father and mother, James and Pearl Cauldwell had given them a house and his father and mother, John and Caroline Newburg had paid for Mary Ellen to pick out the furniture she wanted.

Edward was so glad she didn't want him to help pick out furniture. She said she and her mother would do it. How good is that he thought. He was not looking forward to that at all, and was glad she and her mother were doing it.

He longed to be with Juanita so much it hurt. He would call her every chance he got, but hearing her sweet voice was all he needed to make him so sad that he had to work at not letting it show. He really wished he could just tell them all to go fly a kite but he knew that if he did, there would be all kinds of fallout. His Dad said if they didn't merge the two companies he didn't know what would happen to the business he had started when he was young and had worked so hard to get it where it was now, and didn't want to lose it because Edward was being stubborn. His mom, Caroline would cry and say he was ruining her life. He just had no choice He was not worried about money. In a few months he would be able to collect his inheritance from his grandfather.

CHAPTER FIVE

WHEN THEY GOT home from their brief honeymoon, and got to their house, Edward's mom had moved all his things to the new house and Mary Ellen s' mother had done the same for her. He was a married man now and after a few days, he told his wife he had to go on a business trip with one of his friends to see about an investment they might want to make together. Mary Ellen was fine with that, as she and her Mother were planning her first big party.

As soon as he left, he called Juanita and told her he was on his way to see her. She was overjoyed to hear that he was back from his business trip and would be home soon.

He wanted to get her a gift to surprise her. He decided he would get her a locket that he had seen and admired when he was at the pawn shop. He could show her how she could open it and put their pictures in it. She would like that, he thought.

When he got to the shack which was no longer a shack, he was happy with the results of the renovation. They were not quite finished, because there had been so much to do.

Most of it was done though, leaving just a lot of cosmetic things to do. He loved the way Juanita looked but most of all, how she looked at him and hugged him like she would never let go. She looked so happy and when he told her he had a surprise for her, her eyes just sparkled and she said I too have a surprise for you. He said to her, my surprise first. He gave her the locket and showed her where she could put the pictures in it. She loved the locket and told him that one of the teachers in the orphanage had a locket that opened like that and she had wanted one ever sense she first saw it. He put it around her neck and fastened it. She looked at him and smiled so brightly.

She said, now I will give you my surprise. She brought out a gift wrapped in some of the tissue paper she had saved from one of her gifts from him. As she handed it to him, he thought it must be something she had knitted for him because it was real soft. When he opened it, he got the surprise of his life. He certainly didn't expect what he found. He held it up and it was a little pink sweater. He said "it might be a little too small for me" and laughed. She blushed and said are you happy? He finally realized what she was trying to tell him. He was so shocked he was speechless. She started to cry and said, you don't want it? He went to her and said "Honey, the sweater won't fit me but I like it and I love what it means". I'm sure it will fit our child. But what if it's a boy? At this point, she smiled her terrific smile and handed him a blue sweater just like the pink one. He grabbed her and swung her around and hugged her so tight that there was no doubt how he felt about it.

He had planned to stay a few days with her and when they went to bed that night, he lay awake long after she had gone to sleep thinking about the future and wondering how he was going to handle it. Mary Ellen was becoming a bigger problem than he first thought.

He enjoyed a few days with Juanita. He was so thrilled that she was carrying their first child. He so wanted to be with her all the time and have a wonderful life with her and raise children with her. He just had to figure out some way to do this and still do what his mom and dad wanted him to do to help their business. He knew it wasn't fair to Juanita or to Mary Ellen, and not even to himself. He was going to have to go back to attend Mary Ellen s' big party soon, but as soon as it was over, he would be back here to his home with Juanita.

CHAPTER SIX

WHILE DRIVING BACK to Indianapolis, he thought of how he was going to manage his life. Mary Ellen didn't seem to miss him while he was gone. She was so intent on playing the society lady that she hardly had time to know he was missing. This was a good thing. His mom and dad didn't miss him because they thought he was with Mary Ellen enjoying wedded bliss. Also, they had their mind on other things just now. Edward's mother's sister and husband, Elaine and John Pierson who were in China as medical missionaries. They were coming for a visit and to bring their daughter Grace Lynn to stay with them while finishing her education at university. It also gave Caroline Newburg the daughter she never had, to fuss over and enjoy, so she was making lots of plans.

Edward really had started a business with Thomas Jenkins and part of the time he legitimately was away on business, but it was close to his home so he could stay at home and be with Juanita. He now had his computer set up there and had an office in their home. Most all his business could be done there. This gave him lots of time to be with Juanita. He cherished any time he could have with her.

As he neared Mary Ellen's house, (he didn't think of it as his home) in Indianapolis, he arrived there late at night. He went to bed in the guest room so as not to disturb Mary Ellen. He awoke the next morning to hear his wife being very sick in their bathroom. He went in to see about her and she told him she had been doing this for a while and her mother had taken her to the doctor and he said she could expect her baby in about seven months. He didn't know what to say to her. She swore she was on the pill because she didn't want children right away. Well he too didn't want children right away but there was no changing this now, he told her.

She told him she was not going to have this baby if the doctor would do an abortion. She didn't want to lose her figure now. The doctor said she had to get the husband's signature first before he would perform the abortion. As much as Edward did not want a child by her, he would not let her kill his child. He was strictly against abortions. He tried to reason with her but she was adamant. He said he would not sign the paper for her to have their child killed. She said "when did you become so religious?" He tried to tell her it wasn't a religious thing but it was killing a person and that was wrong. She laughed at him and said she would take care of it herself.

Being her mother's only daughter and used to having her way, her mother gave in to her. When they went to see the Doctor that her mother had found to do it, he refused to do it too because he said she had waited too long and it was not a viable procedure to do now. Mary Ellen was livid and told Edward to get out and she never wanted to see him again. She threw a temper tantrum and threw all his clothes out in the garage. She started to throw them out the front door until she saw her neighbor looking and changed her mind and put them in the garage. He packed his suitcase and left that evening.

Her father was angry with her but he wasn't too worried about the business as the merger had already taken place and was going well. That left Edwards' father to contend with but when Edward talked to his dad his dad said he recognized that Edward had been unhappy with her and he should just go ahead with his own life and run his new business with his friend and let things settle down. This was fine with him.

CHAPTER SEVEN

H E WENT TO the shack, as he still called it, to see Juanita. She didn't know he was coming and was so happy to see him. She was like a breath of fresh air to him after what he had been through. They spent the next few days just doing nothing but getting to know each other more. It was like a honeymoon to them.

He enjoyed watching her animation as she showed him her pictures she had taken with her new camera. They went shopping for new things for the house, now that it was finished. Juanita tried to tell Edward that the old furniture they had been living with was good enough but he wouldn't hear of it. They furnished each room with new furniture. He finally was getting her to open up and tell him when she liked or disliked something. He found that she had exceptionally good taste. It took them about a week of shopping every day to get everything done, but it was a beautiful home when they were finished. Edward told Juanita that now since they had their house finished and were truly making a home of it, they should name it and put up a sign. Juanita laughed at him until she realized he was serious. She said "Do people really name their houses?" He told her not all people do but they like to do that if the house holds a lot of meaning to them. Juanita said then we shall name our house because it and you mean everything to me, and you already have a name. What shall it be Edward? He answered her, "anything you want it to be. I'm not very good with names." Juanita thought for a minute and smiled as she said, I have the perfect name. Our house should be called EDNITA MANSION, using part of both names. So it was settled. Edward told her he would have a very nice sign made soon.

In the next few days Edward was busy getting the sign made and was just getting it hung over a very pretty gated archway, leading to their house. Edward had gone all out and had a beautiful wrought iron fencing made to go with the elegant archway and gate. He said a name like this called for a nice place to put it. It did so much to enhance the beauty of their home. Edward said he would have to quit calling it the shack now. As they were going inside after admiring the sign, his cell phone rang and when he answered it, his mother asked him to come home for a family dinner on Saturday. He wanted to make an excuse but then his mother told him his cousin Grace was there and would be staying with them. He knew he had to be there for Grace. He hadn't seen her for four years and she was in university now. He really did want to see her. They were always very close.

At home he had a good time renewing his cousinship (as he used to joke and say) with his cousin Grace. Then he was summoned to his father-in-laws' home to talk. He knew Mary Ellen was getting a divorce and he would not try to stop her. He couldn't figure out what they wanted to talk about.

But he went at the time they asked him to come. He didn't know what awaited him but he was ready for just about anything. The news was his father-in-law telling him Mary Ellen and her mother had left for Europe so Mary Ellen could recuperate from a miscarriage she had just had. Edward asked him if it was really true. He begged him to please tell him the truth. His father-in-law was more honorable than his wife. He said he believed they just told the story of losing the baby and since she could not get an abortion, they were going to let people here believe she had a miscarriage but was really going to try to get an abortion or let the baby be adopted. Edward was appalled at her lies and trickery and asked where they had gone but they had kept it a secret from everyone. He just didn't know. Edward was truly sad but did not know anything to do to get his child back. He decided to concentrate on Juanita and their child.

CHAPTER EIGHT

W HEN HE WENT back to see Juanita, he went to the
doctor with her and then they went to buy nursery
furniture. Juanita was overjoyed at all they bought for the
baby, the doctor said she would probably give birth in one
month. When he asked if they wanted to know what the sex
of the baby was now, Juanita said very excitedly "no! That is
Gods secret and not ours to know until the baby is born."
Edward put his arms around her to comfort her because she
was so upset. He didn't understand what upset her so. She
told him when he asked why she was so upset about it, that
the Baby is not theirs yet but when it is born, then is the
time to meet Gods' gift to them and get to know their child.
Edward said that was fine with him and he understood. This
pleased her and she was content to wait to see her baby when
it was Gods time.

Edward wanted to bring his cousin Grace out to meet
Juanita. He knew if he asked Grace to keep his secret, she
would say nothing to anyone. He felt he ought to prepare
her first. So he told Juanita he was going to bring his very

special cousin out to meet her. When he went home to get his cousin, he told his mother he wanted to take Grace for a few days to see some of the pretty land and to introduce her to some of his friends a little ways away. She was glad that he was taking an interest in Grace and told them to have fun and be sure to be back in time to start to school. They laughed and said they were sure they wouldn't be gone that long.

When he was alone with Grace, he told her he wanted to have a long talk with her and then he wanted her to meet someone. But first, he said, you must promise me that you will not reveal what I am about to tell you to anyone. Grace told him he could trust her to tell no one, as long as it would not hurt anyone. He agreed to that. Then Grace told him how sad she was when she heard that Mary Ellen was divorcing him. He said that is part of what I want to talk to you about.

When he started to talk to Grace, it was like a fountain of words started flowing from him and as he talked, it was as if a heavy load rolled off him. He was not sure what to call it. Was it grief, or anger, or gladness or sadness? He just didn't know what, but he had kept this bottled up inside of him with no one to talk to about it and now here was Grace, ready to listen and not judge him for choosing wrongly. Grace was a true Christian girl and she told him. "If you don't mind, I would like you to find a place where we can stop the car for a while and pray about this. Edward told her he had not said one prayer since he was a little boy and prayed "now I lay me down to sleep" like when we were little. He said he didn't know how. Grace told him he didn't have to pray, but she would like to pray for him. He agreed that it might help, so they pulled over on to the side of the road where there was a pull out for cars to stop for a while or even turn around. They had been driving for quite a while and he was ready for a break anyway. He turned to Grace and asked her to pray that God would watch over his child that was being adopted and give him or her good Christian parents. Grace bowed her head and prayed first for the missing child. Then she prayed for Edward that he would find peace in his heart by getting to know God better and to know what blessings He could give and peace that would pass all understanding. And then she prayed for Juanita, who she hadn't met yet. She asked God to guide them all in ways to straighten out his tangled web that had become his life. She asked it in the name of Jesus. When she was finished, she looked at Edward and saw that he was softly crying. He told her he loved Juanita so much and was so sorry that he had tried to make her think that they were married. Grace said you know there is a very easy fix for that.

CHAPTER NINE

WHEN THEY ARRIVED at Edward and Juanita's home, Edward introduced Grace and Juanita. There was an instant bond forming between them. They had one thing in common, they both loved Edward. Juanita, as his wife and Grace as his cousin. Grace talked a bit to Juanita about God. She wanted to see where Juanita stood. She asked her if she had asked God to come into her heart and to live her life as God would have her do. Juanita answered her with this question. Someone came to the orphanage once and told us we should do this but I didn't understand. Would you explain it to me? Grace read to her in the Bible in Romans 10:9. If you confess with your mouth "Jesus is Lord" and believe in your heart that God raised Him from the dead, you will be saved. When Grace finished reading, she asked Juanita if she believed this. She said yes, she did. Then Grace said then why don't you just pray and ask God to forgive your sins and make your heart clean and come into your heart. Juanita did this and then Grace explained to her that she can talk to God any time she wanted to and about anything and He will hear and answer her. She explained to her that if it seemed like God didn't answer her, it might be it was not time yet. Or maybe it would not be good for you to have what you have asked God about. She explained to her, it is the same as if a child asks his earthly father for something and the father knows that it would not be good for that child to have this thing now and so he would not give it to him. We should always remember to want Gods' will and timing in things for He knows what is best for us. He knows the future and we don't. Grace told her that in Jeremiah 29:11 it says "For I know the plans I have for you", Declares the Lord. "Plans to prosper you and not to harm you. Plans to give you hope and a future".

When she finished reading, she looked at Juanita and she was smiling. She said, "then all I have to do is trust God and love him". Then Grace looked at Edward and he looked so sad and had tears in his eyes. He said "why did I not know this before I made such a mess of my life, when it would have helped me?" Grace told him there was nothing to stop him now. She told him that even if he had made a mess of his life so far, there was nothing that was too hard for God. She helped him to pray and ask God into his heart and to forgive his sin. He cried out to God and asked Him to guide him in fixing the wrongs he had done. There was rejoicing in three people's hearts in that house that day.

Grace knew she was going to have to get back to her Aunt's house to get ready to start to school. She had one more thing she wanted to do before she went back. She was sure once she got started in school she would not have a lot of time for she was planning to carry a full load of credits once she started. She talked to Edward in private and asked him if he planned to marry Juanita now. He said yes he was and the sooner the better for he wanted to do this before the baby was born. They talked to Juanita and she agreed to do it any time they wanted to. Juanita started to refer to it as her really real wedding.

Grace went with Juanita to buy a pretty dress. It was a maternity dress that was just beautiful on her. While they were busy doing this, Edward was buying her a wedding band with three diamonds in it. It was just the kind he wanted for her. He also spoke to a minister and told him the details of the circumstance they were in. The minister said he would like to set up a time when he could talk with them and then he would see about a time for the marriage. When Edward told him he would like to talk to him today if he had the time for time was of the essence as Juanita was due any time to have her baby. He said "well how about right now if you are both here." Edward said he was supposed to meet them in fifteen minutes and he could call his cousin on her cell phone and tell her to meet them at the church. This was working out perfectly because his friend Mitch was with them as they had met him just a little while ago, not even knowing he had planned to be in town.

Mitch and Grace had known each other from when Grace had been visiting before. They were talking about what each had been doing since they had last met. When Edward called Grace, he explained to her what he planned and asked her if she could get Juanita to wear her new dress and meet them at the church as soon as possible. She said was it okay if Mitch came along? Edward said by all means because he thought that after the pastor had talked to them they could get the wedding vows said and Grace could be the maid of honor and Mitch could be best man. Grace promised to meet them as soon as she could get them there. She had one stop to make after she got Juanita into her new dress, and had explained what was going on to Juanita and Mitch. Mitch said what a good thing he was dressed for the business meeting which was what had brought him here today. Grace stopped at a florists and had the florist make up a beautiful wrist corsage for Juanita to wear. The florist said she hadn't had a call for a wrist corsage in years, but she would make it. She said, when she finished it she quite enjoyed making it. Grace thought that a wrist corsage would be better for Juanita in her condition. She was glad she thought of it for it worked out perfectly.

The pastor, after talking to the two of them and knowing from his talk that they had both become Christians, said he would be glad to perform the ceremony now. His wife came out and asked if they would like to have music and they both shook their heads yes. The pastor's wife, Mary Moore said she would like to sing and accompany herself on the piano singing a very old love song that was a favorite of hers. When she started to sing, she sung the old song," I Love You Truly" in a beautiful voice. Both the bride and groom were mesmerized as she sang. They thought it had the most meaningful words that suited them perfectly. When the pastor pronounced them husband and wife and told

Edward he could kiss his bride, he felt like his dream had finally come true. After the ceremony was finished, the pastor invited them to come to his church Sunday. They said they surely would

CHAPTER TEN

THE WHOLE WEDDING party went to a nice restaurant for dinner and all had a wonderful time until they looked at Juanita as she made a strange little noise. She said I think the baby wants to see his mama and papa tonight. They all laughed at her strange way of saying things, until they realized she was telling them her baby was trying to be born now. They all rushed out of the restaurant until Mitch realized they hadn't paid the check. He waved them on and said he would catch up to them at the hospital. There was only one in their little town so he knew where they would be. Juanita had her little boy soon after they got to the hospital. Everyone was congratulating the father as the Doctor came in and asked for Edward to follow him. They all were so afraid that something had gone wrong with either Juanita or the baby. They started to pray for them right away. Edward said, is my wife alright can I see her now? The doctor said I think you can see her soon but maybe you would like to see your little girl first. Edward said, I already saw our baby and even got to hold him but we had a little boy. The Doctor said yes, I know you have a boy but you also now have a girl. Edward had to sit down in the nearest chair he could find. He was in shock. The doctor said, we suspected there night be another one hiding there but Juanita was so adamant about no more tests, no more! We thought we had better let well enough alone. She was not in any kind of danger nor were the babes.

When he saw Juanita, she had a baby in each arm and was smiling so bright he was sure she could outshine the sun. She said she was ready to go home now but the doctor said it would be a few days yet before they could go home, but Edward could visit them every day. He stayed until they shoved him out the door

When they brought the babies home, Edward wanted to get her help in caring for the babies but Juanita was so offended to think he didn't think her capable of caring for them. He gave up and said he would work at home and he could watch the babies to let her have a rest now and then. Grace had to go back to her aunts so she could start to school. Edward did talk Juanita into letting him hire a girl to come in twice a week to clean the house. She agreed as long as they didn't touch the babies.

After Grace left, Edward, Juanita and the babies were living quietly in their home. There was a little controversy over names, when Edward teasingly told Juanita "oh just call them Jack and Jill". But they soon settled on Gloria Grace and Maxwell Mitchell, after their maid of honor and best man at their wedding. That was soon shortened to Glory and Max. They did start to go to church regularly and the pastor asked them if they wanted to have a dedication service for their children. They neither one knew what he meant and he explained that it was just a time when they brought the babies to the front of the church and the pastor would ask them to promise to teach their children to know God and to bring them to church and pray for them. They would promise to do that and then the pastor would pray for both parents and babies. He also would ask the congregation to promise to pray for the new parents too. Edward and Juanita both wanted to do that. There was a date set. Edward was thinking more and more how he could tell his parents about his marriage. He knew that he should have taken care of this long ago and he regretted that his parents didn't even know they had grandchildren. He was praying that God would show him the way to tell them. He would like them to be at the dedication of the babies.

CHAPTER ELEVEN

NEW ZEALAND
Charley and Mollie Neilson

C HARLEY AND MOLLIE Neilson lived just out of the town of Auckland, New Zealand. They had a small sheep ranch. Charley was a tall man and very muscular from doing his work with the sheep. Mollie was a tall willowy redhead. Charley had told her he was going to marry her when he first saw her in the first grade at school. Then when he saw her again at church, he leaned over to his mother and told her he was going to marry that girl with the wild red hair sitting two rows in front of them. His mother was trying to shush him up as his dad frowned at him, but he just smiled at them as if he knew a secret. He was all of six years old then.

They started to date in high school and had eyes for no one but each other since. Their work load greatly increased at sheering time. But they loved their life and their working dog, Jimbo, who they called Jim. He was as important a part of the sheep ranch as any man would be. He had a very important job to do to roundup the sheep. Their nice little spread kept them busy but they loved it.

Charley was assistant Pastor at their church and Mollie played the piano for the children's choir. They were kept quite busy with their sheep raising and their church work. There was just one thing lacking in their otherwise happy life. They were childless. They had prayed for so long for God to let Mollie conceive and bear them a child. But He had not seen fit to give them children. Now at this time in their life they were looking into adoption. They had talked to a Doctor James Hedridge, who was a member of their church and who handled private adoptions. He told them that quite often an individual would seek his help to find a good home for an unexpected or unwanted child. He told them he would keep his ears open and also ask his colleagues if they knew of anyone seeking a home for an unborn child. Now they just had to wait and pray that God would provide in His time and if it was His will for them to become parents. They felt sure they were meant to be parents or God would not have put such a burning desire in their heart.

CHAPTER TWELVE

MARY ELLEN AND her mother had arrived in New Zealand and were at the Auckland Airport. They had arranged to have a limousine to take them and their luggage to their hotel. Their ride to the hotel was not there and Pearl Caldwell was tired and angry. She was angry at her daughter for getting her into this situation and angry at the transportation system for not being more prompt and angry at God for letting this happen. She was glad that her grandchild was not going to be killed. She was all for the abortion at first but thinking it over, she was glad that they had waited too long to get the abortion. Now, at least, her grandchild would have a life with caring parents. That is what the doctor had promised.

They were to meet with the doctor tomorrow. Mary Ellen was still sure that they should have tried for the abortion. She had no feeling for this child she was carrying. What kind of a child had she raised? She just didn't understand her and yet Pearl knew it was her fault and knew she was not a good mother. How could her daughter have been a good mother with her as an example? Maybe it was Gods' plan for that baby to have better parents than what it would have staying with them.

In the middle of the night. Mary Ellen woke her mother and said her water had broken. This meant that Pearl must call the doctor and he would get in touch with the adopting parents. Then she must get her to the hospital. The doctor that was handling the birth was also the one to take care of getting the attorney that is doing all the paper work for them. Pearl was glad it would soon be over.

Dr. Hedridge called the Nielsons in the middle of the night to tell them they should go to the hospital. He had told them of the girl who wanted to have her baby adopted when it was born. She had refused to let them tell her the sex of the child and she didn't want to hold or see the baby. She had made the remark that she wanted no part of the whole process. She just wanted to get the birth over with so she could go to a spa and start to get her figure back so she could go home and live her life and forget this ever happened. Dr. Hedridge was also glad it would be over soon, for he had never met such a cold young person as this girl. He knew that this baby would have a good Christian home and would be loved.

The Nielsons had been overjoyed when Dr. Hedridge first called them. They had been preparing for the baby ever since. They fixed one room as a nursery and the people at church had given a shower for her. She and Charles had been so happy and excited. Now the time had really come that they would have the child that God was giving them.

They were glad they didn't know the sex of the baby. They had picked out a name for either a boy or girl. If it was a boy they would name him John Paul. If it was a girl, she would be named Hannah Ruth. They were on their way to the hospital now. Mollie's parents Russell and Mable O'Brian were visiting from Minnesota and would be there to see their first grandchild and also Charles' parents, Adam and Martha Nielson who lived close by would be there to welcome their first grandchild into the world, but the Doctor said he would like for only the Nielsons to be there.

When Mary Ellen and her mother got to the hospital, they whisked Mary Ellen off and Pearl went to the room where they told her she could wait. The nurse was so nice to her. She could see that she had no one to wait with her. She knew a little about the circumstances and her heart went out to the sad woman. She asked her if a cup of coffee would be good while she waited and Pearl was so thankful and said yes that would be great. The nurse brought her a cup of steaming coffee and had cream and sugar if she wanted it. She stayed with her as long as she could but she had to get back to work as her shift was not over yet.

The Nielsons were taken to another part of the hospital so the adoptive parents would not be known. Mary Ellen asked them to give her something so she wouldn't feel the pain. The doctor told her she had work to do to bring this baby into the world. She didn't like that but when the pains got harder, and the doctor told her to push, she began to co-operate with them and she actually had a quick delivery. But to hear her tell it, she suffered like no one else had. Hers was a terrible delivery and she would make sure she never had to go through that again.

When they brought the baby to the Nielsons, they handed the baby to Mollie and said here is your little boy. He is a large little guy He weighed Eight pounds, two ounces and is twenty inches long. The mother and father looked at him and said "hello John Paul, welcome to our family"

Pearl had planned to take Mary Ellen on a tour of Europe as soon as she was recuperated enough, but Mary Ellen said no way. As soon as I am able to travel I'm going home and throw the biggest party I can. Her mother was stunned at this but said nothing. She would do what her daughter wanted to get her home and get some peace for herself.

CHAPTER THIRTEEN

INDIANA

Edward and Juanita had been talking and praying about how to approach this thing with his parents. Edward's parents had no idea he owned a home. They didn't know he was married. They didn't know they were grandparents to twins. Two delightful laughing twins who were identical in every way except one was a sweet little girl and the other was a sweet little boy. How could they not forgive them for keeping it a secret once they saw those sweet kids? They had become very involved in their church and had asked the church to pray that God would lead them in the right way to go about giving this information without it hurting his parents so.

Edward thought it would be better if he talked to his parents alone first. It might be less of a shock. He called his parents and asked if he could come and take them out to dinner? He said he had something to talk to them about.

They said "sure son, we would be glad to go to dinner. When did you have in mind to go?" How about tomorrow night at our favorite restaurant? His Mom and Dad knew where he meant so they said they would meet him there at whatever time he chose. Edward said how about seven, and they agreed that would be good for them. So now all Edward had to do was pray a lot and try to be calm and let God handle the situation and tell him how to say what he had to say to his parents.

When Edward left to go see his parents, he prayed all the way. They were so glad to see him and at his invitation too. They were so used to having to summon him home to get to talk to him about anything. Now here was their son asking to meet them. They were not fooled by this though they knew he wanted something. They laughed on their way over to the restaurant and said how much money you think he will want this time. They didn't mind though, for they felt he was growing up a little. When they got to the restaurant and were seated, his dad started to speak. Edward put his hand on his dad's arm and said "Dad, let me speak first before I lose my nerve."

His mom immediately said "son, what is wrong?" He was quick to assure them that nothing was wrong, except he had kept a secret from them and now he was here to make it right even if he was late in doing it. His mom and dad both looked at him questioningly. He said I don't believe I know where to begin. His mom patted his hand and said, son, just start at the beginning. Edward said, I believe that is where I will start.

Dad, Edward began, you remember when you offered me a trip to where ever I wanted to go and when I said Mexico you were surprised and tried to change my mind? John Newburg looked at is son and said, I remember. Edward said now I would like to tell you the story of my life starting from that time until now and then I will answer your questions. Is that ok with you? They both shook their heads yes.

Edward started his story. "I went down to Mexico not with any one and not with anything in mind to do. I think I knew you wanted me to go someplace in Europe and I just wanted to do my own thing. When I got there I was so bored so I just roamed around in town for a while and was about ready to come back home. Then I saw this beautiful girl that looked lost and frightened, and hungry. I thought she might be afraid of something. She looked very young and when I tried to talk to her she shied away from me. I kept trying to talk softly and not to seem threatening, and finally she didn't back off from me anymore. I asked her if she was hungry but she wouldn't answer me then I kept talking to her and told her I was on vacation from the United States and would have to go back soon but I wanted to get something to eat and I didn't know the best place to eat and if she could show me maybe she would be hungry enough to eat with me and keep me company. She shook her head and got up to follow me.

From that time on, she was my shadow. I found out later that she hoped to get to the United States because she was told that is where her mother went when she left her at the orphanage. He told them how he had brought her back with him and of their marriage and then of their twin grandchildren. He told them how he and Juanita had both joined the church and were saved when Grace read the bible to them and that he had a home that he owned and that is where they lived. Then he asked them the question that he had been dreading. Will you forgive me for being so foolish and thinking I had to keep it a secret from you?

They both, with tears in their eyes said they would forgive him if they could see their new daughter-in-law, and two new grandchildren. They made arrangements to come to Edward and Juanita's' house tomorrow. They said they would start right after breakfast and Edward asked them if they would come prepared to stay a few days with them and get acquainted with his wife and son and daughter. They said he might have to push them out the door to get rid of them when they got hold of those grandkids.

They left to go home and bask in their good news. Edward went home thanking God for bringing him through this in such a wonderful way. When he came through the door at home, Juanita saw the smile on his face and knew that everything was right with his mom and dad. She was so happy for him for she realized how afraid he was that his parents wouldn't forgive him.

The next morning John and Caroline were up early and preparing to go to stay with their son and his family for a few days. This was as foreign to them as anything they had ever done. One thing that had happened to them while Grace was staying with them, was a renewal of their faith in God. Over the years, they had let themselves drift away from going to church. They were so busy in their business and had even let that business make them push their son into a loveless marriage and that was their fault. How they had come to regret that decision! But they had repented to God and asked His forgiveness and now they were right with God and walking with Him and asking His guidance in their life instead of going their own way.

Now they had found that their son had also come back to serving God again. They decided this morning that they were so excited about going to see those babies that they didn't want to take time to cook breakfast so they just packed their bags and got ready to go, deciding they would eat breakfast on the way. They had a favorite little café they loved. So they would just stop there to eat, and then be on their way. When they were seated in the restaurant at Marie's table, as was their regular place, they couldn't wait to tell her about their grandchildren. She told them to please bring pictures of them on their way back home. They assured her they would have plenty to show her. About an hour after they got on the road again, they were nearing the turnoff to go to Edwards home.

They marveled that their son had bought this place and realized that they had been so lost in their own affairs that they had neglected to keep in touch with their sons' doings. They knew they had failed him in some way if he had kept this big secret from them because he was afraid to tell them. He must have been afraid of their disapproval so much.

When they pulled up in front of the house, they were so amazed that their son had such a beautiful home. Juanita had been busy planting flowers all around and she had Edward get her some big potted plants to sit on both sides of the porch, right at the top of the stairs. They were stunned at the beauty of the fence with its archway with the beautiful sign over it. They loved the name that included part of both names to make one. They were truly joined in all ways. Their son had done all this without their help. They were so proud of him. Almost before the car stopped Caroline was out of the car, so excited was she to meet her new family members. They were all there waiting for her.

Edward was holding a squirming Max and Juanita was holding a wiggling Gloria, who they had started to call Glory. Grandpa took one baby and grandma took the other. They hugged and kissed them and then they traded and did the same to the new one they held. Edward put his arm around Juanita, and brought her to his mom and dad. He said Mom, Dad, I want you to meet my wife. She is the love of my life. Then he turned to Juanita and said Honey, I want you to meet the best mom and dad a guy like me could have. Caroline and John held the baby with one arm and put the other one around Juanita. John said "welcome to the family from both of us". They stayed a few days and just couldn't take enough pictures and didn't really want to leave. They were there for the Sunday the babies were dedicated. They were so proud to be asked to take part in the service. They were even more proud of their son and his family. They made plans for Juanita and Edward and the babies to come for Thanksgiving to their house. They would then make the trip to their sons' for Christmas. They knew the Holidays were going to be great and they thanked God for all the blessings He had given them this day. On the way home, they talked together as never before about how they thought Edward should marry Mary Ellen and how they had almost ruined Edwards' life by insisting he marry her. They knew now how wrong they were.

CHAPTER FOURTEEN

NEW ZEALAND

WHEN THE NIELSONS were given their baby boy to hold, they were the happiest couple around. They had signed all the necessary papers already and now they would have to leave him here until tomorrow. It was hospital policy to leave him in the hospital overnight. They had a room all fixed up for him at home. They had been working on it since they first heard they would get the baby. It was a beautiful nursery. They couldn't wait to take him home tomorrow and introduce him to his Grandpa and Grandma Neilson and Grandpa and Grandma O'Brian. Then of course he would be introduced to Jimbo, the herder dog. Then he would be enrolled in the nursery at church and be on the cradle roll until he got older. They planned to have the dedication next Sunday. They were so excited with all the holiday in the offing and all that meant. This was the best time of the year. It would soon be warm enough to really romp in the sun with John Paul. Then with Christmas coming, maybe John Paul could play the part of Baby Jesus in the Christmas pageant.

The O'Brians 'thought it was such strange weather here because they were from Minnesota in the United States and it was very cold there at this time of year, but it was summer here. They didn't know if they could ever get used to it here. They wouldn't have to try it though, as they would be leaving soon to go back to Minnesota. They sure hated to leave their first grandson. They had brought a very nice camera with them as a present to the new parents and expected to receive pictures quite often. They had planned to stay through Christmas But they had word from their hands who were looking after their dairy herd that there had been a blizzard and had done some damage and they were needed at home as soon as possible. They would have to depend on pictures for now. Russell and Mable O'Brien left the next morning with tears all around and flew back to Minnesota.

It was such a tiring flight and changing planes twice, they were so tired when they finally got home to Minnesota but they called their daughter and her family in New Zealand to let them know they got home and the dairy herd was safe. They sure missed that grandson though. When they were taking a vacation with their daughter Mollie a few years back, they had no idea their only daughter would meet and eventually fall in love with a New Zealander at a sheep shearing contest they went to see. But Russell and Mable knew there was true love between them and knowing what that meant in their own lives, they would not try to stop it.

Their daughter had been happy with her sheep rancher. The only thing marring their happiness was the lack of children. Now that was solved with Gods' help. They would raise their little John Paul to know God and to trust in him. Maybe they would even teach him the same bible verse we taught her, Jeremiah twenty-nine, eleven. "For I know the plans I have for you declares the Lord plans to prosper you and not to harm you plans to give you hope and a future".

Adam and Martha Nielson were going to get to enjoy every new thing their grandson did for they lived on the adjoining sheep ranch. Mollie laughingly told them she just traded a life on a dairy farm for one on a sheep ranch.

CHAPTER FIFTEEN

Juanita and Edward were enjoying watching their twins, Max and Glory grow. Grandma and Grandpa Newbury called often to find out the latest cute things their grandchildren had done. They were sure Max and Glory were doing everything much before other children their age because they were so smart. They were also very busy showing their pictures to anyone who would have time to see them. One day, the phone rang and when Edward answered, (Juanita still insisted that Edward answer the phone when he was there) She had the idea that if Edward was there It was not her place to answer it. She was so sure who ever it was would want to talk to Edward and not her. When he answered, it was his mother and she had bad news, she said. Edward said, is Dad alright? She assured him his father was fine but their friend and neighbor, Pearl Cauldwell had died of a heart attack last night. She would let them know when the funeral would be. Pearl had been feeling poorly lately and when she would be with Caroline, she kept asking to see the pictures of Max and Glory. She finally told Caroline that she wondered about her own grandchild. She didn't even know if it was a boy or girl. She also explained to Caroline how they had went to New Zealand and Mary Ellen had the baby and the adoptive parents had taken the baby and Mary Ellen didn't even want to know if it was a boy or girl. Caroline said she thought Pearl had died of a broken heart if that was possible. She certainly had been grieving.

Edward was stunned. He was sorry for James' loss, but the news that Edward now had a child in New Zealand was troubling. He loved his Max and Glory so much and now to think he had another child who he might never know was devastating. He was so angry at Mary Ellen that he hoped he would never see her again. He probably wouldn't either, because she and a friend had gone to Europe and when contacted about her mothers' death, she said she had plans that couldn't be changed and didn't know when she would be home. Her father was distraught at her lack of feeling for anyone but herself. He knew she was selfish but he didn't know she could ever behave like this. He felt he had lost a wife and grandchild and now his daughter.

James Caldwell's friends, John and Caroline Newburg were his lifeline now. They were by his side whenever he needed them and were really being a friend and trying to help him through this awful time. He had no one else. When Edward heard this, he felt such sorrow for James Cauldwell. He had always tried to be honest with Edward when the rest of his family had constantly lied to him. He and his family would be at the funeral to try to give what comfort he could to James. The funeral was just before

Thanksgiving, so Juanita and Edward and Max and Glory all went to grandma and grandpas' house and planned to stay for Thanksgiving. Juanita was not sure what this was all about but she was willing to learn. She got right in the kitchen with Caroline and asked her to show her how to make this kind of special dinner. She really enjoyed learning new things. The dinner was wonderful as was the fellowship and camaraderie. The only sad thing was when James Cauldwell would look at Max and Glory his eyes would tear up and you knew he was thinking about his lost grandchild and all his other losses. There were teary goodbyes, hugs and kisses but the young Newbury's had to leave to get back home. Christmas would be here soon and the grandparents would be coming to EDNITA MANSION to spend time with them.

CHAPTER SIXTEEN

T HE NEWBURY GRANDPARENTS had called to see if it was ok to invite James Cauldwell to come along with them for Christmas. Edward said yes, he told them he had been going to surprise them, but he would tell them now. He had his builder build a very nice guest house. It was two bedrooms, each with its own bath, a sitting room and small kitchenette. It was ready for occupancy any time. He said he would call James and invite him personally. His parents thanked him so much for they didn't want to leave him at home alone. He seemed to depend on them so much in his aloneness. His daughter just never even gets in touch any more.

Christmas was a wonderful time for everyone. Even James seemed to brighten and get into the spirit of things. Grandma and Grandpa came loaded with gifts as did James. Of course mom and dad as Santa Clause had done their bit too. Juanita had knitted sweaters for the twins and for Edward. She also asked Edward to take her to the Yarn Store where she bought some beautiful Lavender cashmere yarn and made a sweater for Caroline. The men all had colorful scarves. She had really been working. Edward had bought Juanita a pearl necklace. She cried when she opened it she had said once that she thought pearls were the most beautiful things. He always tried to remember when she mentioned anything and get it for her eventually.

In New Zealand, Christmas was being celebrated at the Nielsons' house. Grandpa and Grandma Nielson were there and a video was taken almost constantly for the O'Brian Grandpa and Grandma in Minnesota. One of the memorable things was when baby John Paul was the Baby Jesus in the Christmas pageant. Never were there any prouder parents than Mollie and Charles Nielson.

CHAPTER SEVENTEEN

(Five years later)

CHARLES AND MOLLIE were so happy watching their son growing so fast and strong. There was just one thing worrying then in their little family. Mollie had been feeling weak lately and not feeling up to par. She had seen her doctor and he took some tests. They were waiting to hear the results. The doctor would not tell them anything for sure. He just said he wanted to see the test results first. He said it could be two or three different things or it could be nothing. Doctor Weston thought of his brother Danny and the struggle he had before his disease weakened him and he caught pneumonia and died. He surely hoped it was not the same disease but it might be. Remembering Danny made him recall that he needed to call Margo, Danny's' wife and see how she and Star were doing. He would do that tonight.

CHAPTER EIGHTEEN

WHEN THE PHONE rang, Margo answered it, and was so glad to hear from her brother-in-law, Thomas Westen. Tom called often to check up on them. Margo loved her little community here in Indianapolis where she had met and married Danny and their Starlita had been born. She was so thankful that she had their little girl Starlita. She was such a comfort to her now that Danny was gone. Star couldn't have had a better Daddy. When Margo had first come to the United States she was married to a man named Frank Summers. At least he said that was his name. He had made her leave her little girl in an orphanage in Mexico. He said he would go back to get her but he was killed just two days after they got married. She had found a job in a nice dinner house and worked to get her citizenship. Then she worked her way up from waitress to head waitress and then as soon as her friend Mary, who was hostess, told her she was getting married and would be moving away, she asked for the job of hostess. She got the job and was so happy for the extra money. She didn't have tips like she used to but the higher pay made up for that and she didn't have to work so hard. Now, when she came home at night she wasn't so tired and could have more energy to do things with Star. She was thinking tonight about how she had met Danny. It was all because she got the new job. She had prayed to God for that job but she didn't know if he would even hear her. She had almost quit going to church and knew she should be taking Star to church. She got the job so she guessed God heard her.

Danny would come into the restaurant and flirt with her a little. Then one day, he asked her for a date. She thought he seemed really nice so she said yes. That was the start of a loving romance. Six months later, he gave her a ring and rushed her into marriage. He said he had plans to go to New Zealand to see his brother and family and friends and he had decided he didn't want to leave her behind. She must go with him.

She remembered that trip so well. The rolling green hills of the North Island with the white sheep on them. One family of their friends had the cutest little boy named John Paul that they had adopted and when they took him to church, they had a poster for each child with their name on it. It was a picture of those green hills and every Sunday they were there, the teacher would give them a sticker in shape of a sheep and they could place it on the hill where ever they wanted. It was so cute watching them do that.

I really wish I could take Star there sometime, and I will. But I want to pay my own way. Tom has offered many times but I just can't let them pay and then stay with them too.

CHAPTER NINETEEN

JUANITA AND EDWARD were enjoying some time alone after the holidays were over and all the guests had left. Juanita told Edward she loved and respected his mother so much but it made her think of her mother and what she was like. How could she leave her child in an orphanage and not come back to get her? Edward tried to explain to her there could be many reasons why she did this. Maybe she was sick or was young and not able to care for a child. There are many reasons that could contribute to her leaving. Edward asked her if she would like for him to look into it to see if he could find any trace of her. Juanita seemed sure she was somewhere in the United States she said oh yes please do. He didn't realize it was bothering her this much. He said he would get on it tomorrow. The next day he had to go into town so he made an appointment to see a private investigator. He met with Bruce Singleton, a friend of his dads who was well known for his work in finding people. Edward gave him all the information he had. Dates and her name as Juanita was told at the orphanage was Margarita Sanchez. He said he would get back with him as soon as he had something to report. Two weeks later, Bruce called and told Edward there was a record of a marriage between a Margarita Sanchez and a man named Frank Summers. He was sure it was the right woman and he was trying to discover what had happened to them. They can't just fade away without a trace. Juanita was very excited at this news. She waited patiently to hear more, but he couldn't find anything more but said he would keep digging. Three weeks went by and he called and told them his report. There had been an accident that claimed the life of one man by the name of Frank Summers. No one else was mentioned.

CHAPTER TWENTY

NEW ZEALAND

Doctor Thomas Weston hated to give the news he was about to give. He had asked Charles and Mollie Nielson to come into his office to talk over the test results He had to give them the news that Mollie had Multiple Sclerosis. He had been pretty sure because of her symptoms His brother Danny had died of pneumonia when he had M.S. He just couldn't fight it off so he had succumbed to it. He told them that with help and proper care she could live to see her boy grow up, but it was imperative that she take proper care of herself.

They assured him they would do everything just as he told them. They asked if they should seek out someone to help her with caring for their boy. They already had a cook and housekeeper. Doctor Weston said he thought she would need someone to monitor her to make sure she had proper diet and rest and if later she had to go to a wheelchair, she would need this kind of help. They asked if he knew of anyone who could provide this help. He said he would check into it and let them know. Above all, they should realize that with proper care she should be able to deal with this. After they left, he thought of Danny again and how Danny was so sure that he could do anything and still overcome this disease. If he had just followed Margo's instructions and taken better care of himself he might have lived a lot longer. He just had that stubborn Weston streak in him and wanted to do it his way. He thought how Margo had trained herself to take such good care of him. She had loved him so. Then he thought maybe that would be the answer to Mollies' needs. He would ask them tomorrow about it. They had met Margo when they were here on their honeymoon. When Doctor Weston spoke to them about Margo coming to help, he explained he had not mentioned it to her yet. They remembered her and liked her very much. Would she move here do you think? Doc said she might, but she would have to live with them and she had a daughter just a bit older than John Paul. Mollie said they certainly had enough room for both of them and it would be nice for John Paul to have a playmate. She would be like a big sister to him.

When Doc contacted Margo about coming to work here and explained it to her, she said she didn't need time to think about it. She would be happy to live in New Zealand and have Star grow up with some of her relatives. So plans were beginning to take shape. But there would be much to do before it would happen. Margo was quite sure it was

Gods will that she should go. She was so lonely here and had been praying that God would show her what to do. The little church she and Star were going to, had been praying for her too. This had to be God working.

CHAPTER TWENTY-ONE

Back in Indiana, Edward got a call from his father. He said there was going to be a wedding soon. Edward couldn't imagine who it could be. His dad said James Cauldwell had been going to church with them and had met a woman named Lacey Adams. They had been a couple going out with John and Caroline to dinner and such. They had decided to get married and planned a simple wedding at the Cauldwell home. They had both been married before and their mates had both died. They just wanted to keep it simple. There would be a sit down dinner that was to be catered. Edwards' mom and dad would be their witness. It would be on Saturday three weeks from today. They were not sending out invitations as it would just be a few friends and family. James had tried to contact his daughter, but Mary Ellen was not answering her phone. This was not unusual as she hadn't talked to her father since she told him she was too busy to come to her mothers' funeral. They left massages for her but had no answers.

Edward and Juanita and the twins went to the wedding and thought it was, as Juanita said "wonderfully beautiful." The ceremony was held in the gazebo with flowers all around. A harpist played soft music as they said their vows. Then they all went in to dinner. Everyone agreed with Juanita, that it was "wonderfully beautiful." The bride and groom went away for a brief honeymoon. Juanita and Edward, Max and Glory stayed overnight with grandpa and grandma, and a good thing they did. The next morning they heard a loud knocking on their door that woke up everyone in the house. It was Mary Ellen demanding to know where her dad was and that gold digging woman he was marrying. She said she was here to stop it before her father made a fool of himself. Everyone was shocked that she would act this way but they all said they didn't know why they were surprised. After all, this was typical Mary Ellen behavior. When no one would tell her where they were she finally left, hopefully going back to England where she said she had been living.

CHAPTER TWENTY-TWO

MARGO WESTON AND her daughter Starlita were busy getting things ready to move to New Zealand. Margo was so glad that she would have employment when she got there and also living arrangements for her and Star. God had answered their prayer in a most spectacular way. He was an awesome God. Star said, "Mommy I think it is just a God thing. He always helps us because He loves us." (Out of the mouths of babes).Yes Star, Margo said. It's like He said in the Bible. Do you remember when we read the other day "and we know that all things work together for good for those who love Him and are called according to his purpose." That is in Romans 8:28.

It didn't take long for Margo to pack up the things that they were going to take with them and some few items they were having shipped. Their apartment was furnished so there was no furniture to deal with. She had given her notice as soon as they were sure they were going and now traveling day was here. They would take a taxi to the hotel today and leave tomorrow morning. Doc Tom, as he was called by his family, had made all the arrangements for them and it was all paid for as part of the job. Their flight left early the next morning but neither of them slept very much after going to bed. They were too excited.

CHAPTER TWENTY-THREE

NEW ZEALAND

WHEN MARGO AND Star left the plane at the Auckland Airport in New Zealand, Margo felt like she was starting a whole new life. She had not been able to get any information about her little daughter that she left at the orphanage so long ago. The orphanage would not tell her anything and she supposed she had been let out of the orphanage at a certain age and was on her own somewhere in Mexico.

She will always regret listening to Frank Summers and letting her baby girl stay in the orphanage in Mexico. She should have been smarter and realize he wouldn't come back to get the baby, but she was so young and didn't know what else to do. When the babies' father was killed before the baby was born she felt so alone. When Frank came along and told her all these lies she had not had enough experience in life to realize when someone was lying to her just to get her to do what they wanted.

When she told the church people about it, they said they would pray for her and for the safety of the little girl, who wouldn't be so little any more. They said that when things seemed impossible, we should turn them over to God and trust Him with all our problems. He cares and understands. He also is the miracle worker. Margo had really tried to turn it all over to God and let Him handle it. Just look how he had got her this wonderful job. In their Sunday school class once the teacher said, "If you see God starting to work on something, don't look away for He probably is just getting started".

Here they were in New Zealand and her Brother-in-law, Doctor Thomas Weston was coming toward them now. She was finally here. They were taken to their new home on the sheep ranch. She met again Charles and Mollie Nielson and now their little boy who was a tiny baby when she last saw him. Now he was bigger than Starlita. They were all introduced around and it seemed like everyone was welcoming them and trying to help them get settled in their new abode. What a great welcoming!

CHAPTER TWENTY-FOUR

Back in Indiana

JUANITA WAS OUT by the lake with Edward and the twins. Edward was just finishing the boat dock he had built. He had bought a pretty new motor boat, a run-about type that would easily have plenty of room for six people. It was his pride and joy. He couldn't wait to take his dad fishing now. His dad had called the other day and asked if he could make plans business wise to take a long vacation. He said he planned to take the family somewhere. Edward had no idea where his dad was thinking about taking them but he had made his schedule to be off for a month. Mitch said he could handle it with no problem, so they were all set to pack up and go as soon as his dad told them where they were going. He was being very mysterious about it. John Newburg called his son and said if they could be ready to go Thursday morning, he and Caroline would be there to pick them up the night before. They would come down Wednesday and stay the night and get an early start Thursday morning. Edward said they could meet them there and they wouldn't have to come all the way down here. His dad said son, just do as I say and don't spoil my surprise. Edward had no idea what his dad was getting at now, but he would do what he said. He was completely mystified.

Edward called his Private Investigator to see if there was an update on Margarita Sanchez before they left for vacation, and to let him know that they would be gone for a while. He still had no word about her. It seemed like he had just come to a dead end. Wednesday afternoon, they heard a vehicle coming down their lane. What they saw was making them all speechless. There was the biggest longest motorhome they had ever seen with his dad and mom sitting in the front seat grinning from ear to ear.

CHAPTER TWENTY-FIVE

WHEN EDWARD AND Juanita saw that motorhome, they knew what the surprise was that his father, John Newburg had been so excited about. They all had a tour of it and Edward asked his dad if he won the lottery or something as those things cost a fortune. His dad told them then, he had decided to retire and so had his partner James, so they had sold the business and bought their retirement home-on-wheels. What a home it was too. It had four pullouts and slept six. There were bunk beds for the twins. His dad said it even had a basement. He showed him where he could store the kids' bicycles and anything they would want. They would load up most of the things today and get up early tomorrow and finish loading with the small things like their toothbrush and be on their way to parts unknown. Edward asked him which direction they were heading and he said he thought east toward Minnesota, but there were many things to see along the way.

James Cauldwell and his wife Lacey were going to New Zealand to visit with Lacey's sister, Martha Nielsen who lives on a sheep ranch there with her husband, Adam. Their son, Charles Nielsen is married to Mollie O'Brian. Mollie's parents Russell and Mable O'Brian, live on a dairy farm in Minnesota. Mollie asked us to stop by her family's dairy farm. She was sure her mom and dad, Russell and Mable O'Brian would love to see them and they could get a head start on getting acquainted, as they would all be vacationing together at Edward and Juanita's this spring. They said they have already called and told them we would be traveling that way in the motorhome, and they would like to meet us, since their plans next year are for the Nielsons, Adam and Martha and Charles and Mollie to visit Mollies' Mom and Dad, but instead of traveling to Minnesota, they will shorten the trip and go to Charles Caudwells place because Mollie will need to rest and not travel on to Minnesota. Mollie has M.S. and she will not be able to travel much longer. So the O'Brians will come here to Indiana to Charles and Lacey's' place to see Mollie and her family. After a short rest, we will all go on to EDNITA MANSION. There is room there for us all to vacation together. Mollie also has someone that stays with her to help her stay as healthy as she can. She sees to it that Mollie eats right and has the proper rest. Her name is Margo. She has a daughter that lives with her named Starlita. They will all be coming. Since we will all be visiting together in Indiana next year. They suggested we might as well get acquainted this year since we will be so close to your home as we travel. They also thought the twins would enjoy seeing the dairy farm. The next morning, they were all up early and ready to start on their exciting trip.

CHAPTER TWENTY-SIX

THE FIRST THING they thought they wanted to see was the Grand Canyon. This was certainly not their first stop though. If they saw something advertised along the road, they stopped to see it if it looked interesting. Sometimes it was great and sometimes it was what they called "a dud", but it was fun being able to stop when they wanted to and eat when they wanted to and wonder of wonders, they didn't have to stop if one of the kids needed to go "right now! Mom". The Grand Canyon was spectacular. And all enjoyed it so much. Even the kids were amazed by it. When Grandpa told them his uncle had actually been with a group who had crossed it from one side to the other on foot, Glory said well it must have taken him a hundred years. Grandpa said he must have felt like it at times

They stopped in New Mexico to see the hot air balloon festival. That, they all agreed was quite a spectacular sight. There was every color of hot air balloon imaginable. The twins both wanted to take a ride in one but Juanita said she would not get in one for anything, Caroline agreed with her, the guys though, said they would be willing to give it a try. They were not offering rides during this part of the festival so the guys were safe in saying this. Caroline secretly told Juanita, John was afraid of heights so she was pretty sure he wouldn't really go, even if he had the chance. They had been on the road for some time now. They all agreed that traveling like this made them feel like they didn't have a care in the world. When they got to Mount Rushmore, and saw the carving of the presidents it raised so many questions from the twins. Max wanted to know how those men got up there to work on them and Glory wanted to know if her daddy thought his head would ever be carved out of a mountain like that.

When they got on the road again, they saw a sign about the carving of Crazy Horse. Everyone thought they ought to see this for sure. This again was spectacular. It was time to go on to see the O'Brians and the dairy farm. When they got started for the day the children were full of questions about the dairy farm. When they were told it was milk cows and a little explanation told to them, they were full of Questions. None of the adults realized the twins had not actually seen a milk cow up close. So as grandpa was trying to explain how the cow is milked, Glory said they squirt it right into the carton? At this point, Edward told his dad he had better wait and let the O'Brians explain it as he was sure they would be milking with milking machines and not the old fashion way. They decided to change the subject.

CHAPTER TWENTY-SEVEN

Arriving at the O'Brians, they were so warmly greeted even though they knew each other only be association to someone else. There was a huge barbeque awaiting them and they all ate the wonderful food and tried to figure out who was who. They figured out the best way to explain it. Russell and Mable O'Brian was mom and dad to Mollie Nielsen. Mollie had met and married Charley Nielsen when the O'Brians were on vacation in New Zealand. Charles, Mollies husband was the son of Adam and Martha Nielsen. Martha Nielson, Mollies' mother-in-law was a sister to Lacey Cauldwell who was married to James Cauldwell, John Newburg's' business partner and friend. Someone asked, then who is this Margo they talk about. Mable O'Brian explained that since Mollie had been diagnosed with M.S. they had Margo move in with them to help take care of Mollie. Charley and Mollies little boy, John Paul now had a playmate because Margo has one daughter and brought her with her to New Zealand when she moved there to take care of Mollie. This seems to be working out very nicely.

Margo knows how to give her proper care, because she took care of her husband Danny Weston, who also had M.S. He had died of pneumonia. Danny Weston was a brother to Doctor Weston, who is Mollies doctor. When Mollie asked him if he could help her find someone who would know how to monitor her rest and diet and help take care of her, He thought at once of Margo. She lived in the United States though so he had to contact her and it has worked out beautifully. She was willing to relocate to New Zealand as long as it would be all right to bring her daughter. It had been good really, Russell O'Brian had said, because now, John Paul thinks he has a big sister.

Mollies' one desire is to see the United States again while she can still travel. Her Mother-in-laws' sister, Lacey Cauldwell who is visiting now in New Zealand, has invited them to come stay with them at the Cauldwell house. They have a big house and lots of room for their family, including Margo and her daughter. They are planning to do this next spring. It will be getting chillier there in New Zealand and nice weather here in the United States. Hopefully we can all get together when that happens, Caroline Newburg said that would be great because, the Caldwells live close to us and Edward and his family live a short drive away. That would be nice for John Paul and Margo's daughter to come play with Max and Glory. Juanita said, no one has called Margo's' daughter by her name. Does anyone know? Oh yes. Forgive us for neglecting to tell you that. She has a very unusual name it is Starlita. Unusual don't you think, but so pretty.

CHAPTER TWENTY-EIGHT

AFTER GETTING THEM all straightened out as to who was who, they had a very pleasant time. They stayed a few days to rest up and then the Newburgs were ready to get on the road again. They all promised to see each other again in the spring.

There was a sign someone saw on the trip about Hollyland. They all thought it would be nice to stop and see a show there. When they got there, there was a dinner show that they thought they would all enjoy, especially the kids. They got tickets and were shown into a big barn of a place with what looked like bleacher seats with wooden plank tables in front of the seats. When they were seated, the show started with some beautiful horses doing things like backing up and obeying the command of the young riders. When they brought the dinner, they were told there would be no forks or knives. They must eat like the cowboys on the range. The kids both thought that would be fun to eat with their fingers. It was actually fried chicken, roasted loaded potato skins, corn on the cob tomatoes quartered, carrot sticks, corncakes, and for dessert, fried peach pies. Milk or iced tea in mason jars. Everyone got a kick out of the dinner and said they would have that at their house sometime. Back on the road they stopped at a few more interesting places, but everyone was getting road weary so they decided to head for home. Edward said he had a few projects he wanted to get started on, and the others could all think of something they felt they had neglected. Also by the time they got home, James and Lacey Cauldwell would be back from their New Zealand Vacation.

CHAPTER TWENTY-NINE

WHEN THEY GOT home, there was the unloading to do and the sorting out of who bought what souvenir from the different places they had stopped at. Then they were all ready to have a good night of sleep in their own bed and grandma and grandpa slept soundly in the big guest house bed.

The next day Edward started to build another house in their back yard. He had promised Max and Glory he would make them a playhouse in the back yard. Max said when he was in it, it would be a club house but Glory said she would have it as a playhouse when she was in it. Max said Dad could you make a sign for it and put it over the door with our names on it? And Glory said Dad could we have a porch on it? Then Max wanted it to be a two story house and Glory said we have to have a kitchen. Edward stopped them and said, Guys, I'll put as many of the things in that you want but there probably won't be everything. Do we agree that whatever I am able to do, it will be ok? They both gave him a hug and said whatever you make will be ok with us.

CHAPTER THIRTY

WHEN ALL THE work was done the look of their back yard had changed drastically. There was a cute little, well, not so little two story playhouse with a porch and windows and a very pretty sign above the door. In the downstairs there was a play sink and a table and chair set. A cabinet with play dishes in it curtains were at the windows. There were three stairs leading up to second floor and there were bed rolls up there. Juanita had to go to town to purchase most of the things but she loved doing it. She found a play stove and a whole set of pots and pans. Dishes Plastic glasses, flatware, She even bought material for dish towels. She bought four bean bag chairs. And a number of books. Edward had made a book case built in. The sign over the door was, "MAX n GLORY" The twins were ecstatic when they got to go into it. Glory moved her baby doll crib in and set her rocking chair on the front porch.

The next thing that Edward started to build was a surprise to everyone. He wouldn't tell them. He said, no, it is a surprise and they would just have to wait. It was kind of a replica of the children's playhouse, but only one story and not nearly so big. It did have a porch on it though. When he finished, he put a nice rug in it and a rug also on the porch. Then he finally came out with the sign he had been making and attached it to the place over the door. The sign said, "Mister McDuffy" Max said "who's he?" and Glory said, he must be a very short man. Edward told them they would have to wait about fifteen minutes, as he looked at his watch. He was secretly afraid he wasn't going to get it done in time. In a few minutes, a truck came rolling down their lane. Edward walked up to greet the man and took something in his hand and opened the door. Out jumped a beautiful Irish setter dog. Edward said, meet Mister McDuffy. He ran to meet everyone with tail wagging and ready to give all he could reach a slurping doggy kiss. Max and Glory showed him his house and Juanita brought out the dishes she had bought at Edwards's instruction when she was in town. She had even had his name put on the dishes and at that, the twins said, you knew about the secret too. She admitted she did but told them someone had to buy him some puppy food too. They couldn't wait to give him a drink. Edward showed them how he had made a special place for his dishes to set so they couldn't be accidentally turned over.

It was such a joyous time getting back home and settling down into a routine. School had started and the twins were in school and loving it so much. They had so much to tell at sharing time in school. The leaves were starting to show that they were soon going to be a variety of colors. Thanksgiving would be the next big Holiday get-to-gather for family and

friends. Last Thanksgiving was at Edwards mom and dad'
John and Caroline Newburg's place, but this year, James
and his new wife Lacey Cauldwell asked if everyone would
come to their place for Thanksgiving. All thought it would
be good, but at the back of everyone's mind was the thought
that James daughter, Mary Ellen might pop in and try to
ruin it for everyone. Caroline told her husband John that
if that did happen, it would be good for all of them to be
there to help James and especially, Lacey. So it was decided
that everyone would be at the Caudwell's for Thanksgiving.

CHAPTER THIRTY-ONE

WHEN THANKSGIVING ROLLED around, the young Newburgs, Edward, Juanita Max and Glory were preparing to go, and they wondered what to do with Mister McDuffy while they were gone. They didn't want to leave him by himself so they were looking into a kennel for him when James called and told them that Mister McDuffy was invited to the turkey dinner too. That being settled, they were all ready to have another fine time together. All were present at the Cauldwells for Lacey's turkey dinner. She was so nervous, because this was her first time doing this. She had always been invited to her mother's house or her late husbands' parent's house for dinner. This was so new to her to do this all by herself. Caroline Newburg had offered to bring something or help in any way she could, but Lacey wanted the full responsibility. She called her sister, Martha Neilson in New Zealand so many times to ask her how to do something that she was a nervous wreck by the time everyone got there. They soon put her at ease telling her how good everything was and complementing her especially on her pumpkin pie.

CHAPTER THIRTY-TWO

AFTER DINNER, THEY were all full of good food and were relaxing in the living room when Mr. McDuffy, also being full, was sleeping between the twins with his head on Glory's lap and his tail slowly switching back and forth while his head was being rubbed, jumped up and started barking and that turned into a growl. They went to see what had caused him to act like that as he had always been so friendly before. In fact, Edward said he will never be a good guard dog for he loves everyone.

Just at that time they heard the door open and Mr. McDuffy lunged toward the door. There was a screech that turned into a scream as Edward got to Mr. Mc Duffy to hold him back. Mary Ellen was in the doorway with a man beside her, He was trying to get her to quiet down but she wanted no part of that. Finally, when she saw that Edward had the dog under control and she wasn't going to be eaten, as she said she thought, she then turned on her father saying is that the way she was treated when she came into her own home? James was embarrassed and nonplussed at the same time.

He was utterly speechless. He had not heard from her in so long. He suddenly found his voice and told her she was welcome to come in to eat. He would have someone fix them a plate of food as there was plenty left, but she must behave herself and quit acting like a spoiled child and introduce her friend. At that, her friend walked up to James, holding out his hand and introduced himself. He said his name was Charles Wingate The third. Mary Ellen quickly interrupted and said He is Earl of Wingate. Max, plowed ahead with his questions. "Well, is he Earl or Charles? Mary Ellen looked at Edward and said I might have known you wouldn't have taught him anything like that. No need as far as I can tell. He'll learn it on his own if he needs to know that. Poor Charles now seemed to be the one nonplussed. But he rallied and said "please excuse my wife." We have had a long flight, and she is tired. So you are married, said Caroline. Our congratulations to you. Please feel right at home.

We invite you to stay a while and get to know the family and friends, said Lacey. We spend a lot of time together and would like you to feel right at home in any of our homes. Mary Ellen looked at Edward and said if you are living in that shack you and Maxwell used to go to fish, I wouldn't take Charles there. Well, Mary Ellen, maybe you ought to come see our shack as you call it. Charles might like to do some fishing. Charles jumped on that right away and said he would love to do some fishing. It was clear to everyone, Mary Ellen did not have him under her thumb as everyone has suspected. He was really a nice sort. Caroline, ever the peacemaker, said why don't we all introduce ourselves to Charles so he can get to know us? Everyone agreed.

Edward stood up and said let me introduce everyone. He started with his dad John then his mother Caroline then Mary Ellen's father James, then he introduced James new wife, Lacey. Then he went to Juanita and put his arm around her and said "this is my sweet wife Juanita and then to his two children and said these are our twins, Maxwell better known as Max and this little lady is Gloria Grace Better known as Glory. Then he went to the dog and said this is Mister McDuffy, better known as Duffy. "Say hi Duffy.", and Duffy sat up and put out his paw. Everyone laughed and Charles said "It's nice to meet you Duffy". He shook his paw. Lacey told Charles that she would show them to their room if he wanted to get their bags. Mary Ellen said that won't be necessary, I think I can find my way to my own room.

It's been a while since you have been here Mary Ellen and we have changed a few things. The guest room is to the right at the top of the stairs and it has its own bath, said Lacey, showing she was the mistress of the house. Well what about my room? Mary Ellen asked. We turned it into James's office so he can work at home. Mary Ellen followed her husband up the stairs without another word. Afterward, Edward and Charles started making plans with James and John to go out on the fishing boat one day next week. When the plans were set, they all said their goodbyes and were on their separate ways home.

CHAPTER THIRTY-THREE

THANKSGIVING WAS VERY different this year. There were a lot of surprises. After everyone left the Cauldwell home, Mary Ellen and Charles said their goodnights to James and Lacey and retired to their room for the night. Charles knew that Mary Ellen was upset and tried to comfort her. She cried in his arms for a while and he asked her to talk to him and tell him what was bothering her. She finally said, "I have hurt so many people including myself. How can I ever make it right?" Charles told her, "You can't make it right Honey until you make it right with God. Do you remember that couple that we met at the airport? They were coming from Africa, retiring from missionary work?" Yes I remember. They turned out to be relatives of the Newburg's and they had their daughter with them who was Edward's cousin and was coming to stay with her aunt while they went back to Africa to help the new missionary couple get started there. Then do you remember what he said to me and how I asked Jesus to forgive me and come into my heart"? Yes I remember, she said. "I did that you know and I have peace and contentment in my very soul"

Mary Ellen said, but you haven't done the hurtful things that I have. Charles told her, Jesus forgives all sin. There is none too great for him and the best thing is if we truly turn from our old ways and follow him, he remembers our sin no more. That's a wonderful thing. Do you really think I could change and be a better person? He answered her, I don't know if you could do that by yourself, but this I do know, that with Gods' help you can. His word says he washes us white as snow. You saw that snow today, it was pure white as it fell to the ground. Why don't you give it a try? I will if you help me, she said. Charles bowed his head and asked God to help him help his dear wife to understand what to do. Then he told her to tell Jesus that you are sorry for the things you have done and ask Him to come into your clean heart and ask his spirit to guide you. Mary Ellen prayed this prayer and looked up to her husband and said I really want to be as good a person as I can be. He told her that none of us are perfect except Jesus, but when we do wrong things and are sorry, we just have to ask God to forgive us and really try to do better next time.

She said do you think the family that I have hurt so will forgive me? Charles told her he felt sure they would because he knew they have Jesus in their heart too. I'm sure you have only to sincerely ask them and they will forgive you as they remember that Jesus has forgiven them, he said. Both Charles and Mary Ellen went to bed that Thanksgiving night, with a light heart.

CHAPTER THIRTY-FOUR

WHEN MARY ELLEN and Charles went down stairs the next morning, she had determined in her heart to first make it right with her father and then with his wife. James and Lacey were already up and were having coffee when Charles and Mary Ellen came into the room. James was steeling himself for whatever came next. Lacey asked if she could get them some coffee. They said a little later please. James was totally shocked when there was no hurtful outburst from his daughter.

Mary Ellen looked at her father with tears in her eyes and walked over to him and put her arms around him and said Daddy I have to ask you something. I want you to forgive me for all the times I have done things to deliberately hurt you. Can you forgive me please? James could not have been more shocked if she had spoken to him in a foreign language. But he welcomed her in his arms. When he could speak, he said daughter, you haven't called me daddy since you were four years old. I don't know what has happened, but yes I forgive you and I want you to know that I have never stopped loving you through all the bad and hurtful times. Since I have been going to church with John and Caroline and got myself right with God I have been praying for you. It would seem like God has answered my prayer.

Mary Ellen then looked at Lacey. Lacey can you ever forgive me for the way I have treated you? Lacey said of course I forgive you and welcome back home Mary Ellen. Dad, Mary Ellen said, there is something I have to tell you now that will be very painful for you and for me too. When we, mother and I went to Europe, we really went to New Zealand. I didn't have a miscarriage as we said. Her father said, I think I knew in my heart you didn't really have a miscarriage. I have lived with your mother long enough to know when she was lying to me.

We went to New Zealand and I had the baby there and gave it up for adoption. James, with tears running down his cheeks said, do I have a grandson or a granddaughter in New Zealand? She said, Dad I don't know. I didn't want to know anything about the baby so I wouldn't let them tell me. I only know its birthday and she told him the date the child was born. Lacey was listening intently.

Mary Ellen said, I realized what I cheated myself and you out of when I saw Edwards's children. And dad, those two kids have a half brother or sister that they will never know. My baby will never know about its half brother and sister. Edward will never get to hold his other child. John and Caroline will never know their other grandchild. Oh, daddy, what a mess I have made with my life and everyone else's. Do you think they will ever forgive me? Child of mine, he said lovingly. With God in control all things can be forgiven.

Soon after that, Lacey asked to be excused and went to her room. She first prayed for God to guide her in talking to her sister and then to guide her sister in what to do with the information she was about to give her. When she dialed her sister, Martha Nielsen, in New Zealand, she had to tell her what she had just learned.

She told her about her step daughter, James's daughter, Mary Ellen. She told her that Mary Ellen had a baby in a New Zealand hospital in the same hospital that John Paul was born and on the same day and had given him up for adoption. Lacey said I believe that John Paul was that baby. It looks as if it is all going to came out as Mary Ellen is asking forgiveness of everyone and there is sure to be a search for that baby. Maybe it is time for Mollie and Charley to tell John Paul he is adopted. I know they were going to tell him when they thought he was ready and maybe this is the right time. Martha Neilson said she would look into it and let her know what was happening from here and would she do the same. They promised to be in prayer about this and keep each other informed.

CHAPTER THIRTY-FIVE

W HEN MARTHA NIELSEN talked to her son and daughter-in-law, they were sure the date was right and on further investigation, they were sure because there were no other baby boys born on that date. In fact John Paul was the only baby born that day. The next thing they did was talk to Doctor Weston and Doctor Hedridge that had handled the adoption. He said it was not a closed adoption because he couldn't get the mother of the infant to listen to anything he said. She was not interested in signing any papers. She said I don't care about anything except getting this over with and getting on with my life. He said he was free to tell them anything they wanted to know. He advised them to tell John Paul about the adoption soon. What they had already surmised was true. Mary Ellen was the mother and Edward Newburg was the father on the birth certificate signed in the hospital by the mother.

When Mollie and Charley told John Paul they had something very important to tell him, he sat up straight as if he knew something important was about to happen. They asked him if he remembered how Mrs. Harper's tummy was big and she told you there was a baby growing inside and that God was forming it and when it was ready it would be born and then she brought her baby to church and showed it to you? His answer was a nod of his head and a serious look in his eyes. He would always get his "I'm paying a lot of attention to you look."

Mommy and I, said Charley, wanted to have a baby so much and we just couldn't seem to have one so we prayed to God to send us a special baby some way. We didn't know how or when it would happen but one day there was a lady who was going to have a baby and she was not able to care for that baby in a good way and she wanted that baby to have a good home and a good Mommy and Daddy.

So God brought us all together and we were able to have you as our baby. You are our son by adoption. That is very special because when we accept Jesus into our hearts, we are in Gods family by adoption. What does that mean for me? Asked John Paul? Well, it means you will always be our son. But you will always have a birth mother and father too. You might even meet them some day but you will still be our son always. His eyes lighted up when he said will I have more grandpas and grandmas too? Yes they said, you have a set of grandparents from your mother and another set from your daddy. Wow He said. John Paul you also have a half- brother and half- sister. He started to speak but they stopped him by saying, and before you ask, they are not half people but they are called that because you all have the same father but different mothers. Will I get to see them some day? Maybe so, they said. John Paul Made a fist and shot it up in the air and said "yea, I'm rich, I've got more family than I can count."

CHAPTER THIRTY-SIX

Indiana

BACK IN INDIANA, Edward, his father John, James, and his new son-in-law Charles had this big fishing day planned. It was planned for the next day so the Cauldwell household was planning to go there today. When they arrived, all was planned where everyone would stay. The guest house had two full suites so James and wife Lacey could stay in one and Mary Ellen and Charles could stay in the other. Edwards's mom and dad could stay in their spare guest room in their house. That took care of everyone.

Each one of the adults noticed a difference in Mary Ellen's attitude. They commented to one another and wondered what had changed her so. The men were going fishing the next morning. They planned to leave early and so they were busy getting the things on the boat so they could pull out early the next day.

Mary Ellen knew she was going to have to wait until they got back to talk to the men, but she wondered if she should try to talk to the women while the men were gone. She asked Charles what he thought and he told her to pray about it and he would too and then just let God lead her. Mary Ellen was not used to praying but that night she poured her heart out to God and asked Him to guide her in what she should say and if she should do it tomorrow with the women.

When the new day dawned the men were soon on their way. The ladies had a leisurely breakfast and were ready to just sit and chat. Mary Ellen asked them if she could talk to them about something that was very serious. They said just say whatever is on your mind. She told them what had happened to her on Thanksgiving night. She said she had asked forgiveness from her father and from Lacey. Lacey smiled at her. She said she would like to ask Caroline to forgive her. Caroline asked her what she wanted her to forgive her for. Mary Ellen then told Caroline what she had done and she was so sorry for keeping her from knowing her grandchild.

Juanita had been quiet all this time. She said now to Mary Ellen. Does Edward know? She told her no one else knows. Just the ones here and the ones she talked to last night. All were silent for a minute and then, Caroline said I do forgive you and I thank you for telling me that I have a grandchild.

When the men got home there was fish to clean and gear to unload but the men felt a different aura about everyone. They knew something was going on. They took care of everything as soon as they could and said tomorrow would be the fish fry. When the men were all showered and cleaned up and they were sitting just telling about the fish they had caught and the one that got away, Charles came to the rescue and said "I believe Mary Ellen has something she would like to say to you". At this, Mary Ellen had all of their attention. She said she wished that they would all forgive her for what she was about to tell them. She looked at Edward and said especially you. She related to them her story of how she had tried to fool everyone by telling them she had a miscarriage. She told them she had gone to New Zealand to have her baby and give it up for adoption. Finally, Edward said, I do forgive you but do you know if there is any way we can know if the child has good parents or not? The doctor had papers for me to sign, something about open adoption but I didn't even listen to him and I didn't sign any papers except the one that said you were the father. Edward, with tears in his eyes, asked, do I have a son or daughter in New Zealand? She said she never knew the sex of the baby. I ask you Edward and you too John to forgive me for keeping your child and grandchild from you. John said I forgive you but Edward said nothing. After a little while, Edward said, Mary Ellen, I have to forgive you, and I do forgive you, but I will try to find out if the child is doing alright and if anything is needed in its life, I will try to provide for it. One thing though, I will never uproot a child from a happy home but I would love to know the child, if that is feasible. At this point, James Cauldwell stood up and said I believe my wife, Lacey, has something to tell you.

CHAPTER THIRTY-SEVEN

LACEY STOOD UP and said, I have sat here and listened to all of you and I think I can clear up some of the questions for you. As you know, my sister, Martha Nielson lives in New Zealand. Her son Charley is married to Mollie O'Brien. You met Russell and Mable O'Brian, Mollie's mom and dad, on your trip to Minnesota this summer. Mollie was not able to conceive a child and wanted one so desperately. They asked God to please let them have a child who needed a home. They didn't care what age. Doctor Weston who is Mollies doctor, said he would look into this for them. He knew Doctor Hedridge who dealt in adoptions and might know someone. Doctor Hedridge told them there was a young lady that wanted to give her baby for adoption as soon as it was born. When the baby was born, it was a boy and they named him John Paul. I heard Mary Ellen when she confessed what she had done and heard the date her baby was born, I called my sister in New Zealand and asked her to check on this. We believe John Paul is your child Edward, and your grandchild Caroline and John. In fact we now know that he is indeed one and the same. There is no doubt now because I have heard from my sister just this morning and she had talked to Doctor Hedridge and he confirmed it and is sending a birth certificate to the father. However, he wished to say that John Paul is so happy with his adoptive mom and dad that he hoped no one would try to uproot him and harm him in this way. They were all overjoyed at this news and swore that they would never do that. Edward asked if it would be possible to meet him sometime. Lacey said, that is the best part of my news. Mollie and Charley had been planning to tell John Paul when they thought he was old enough and at the right time. When they heard my news they thought it was time to tell him.

That little guy took it just so great. He said does that mean what I think? If I have another mother and father somewhere, then I must have another grandparent too. They told him, yes, you have two more sets of grandparents and you also have a half-brother and half-sister. Before he could start asking about the half brother and sister they explained they were not half people but had the same birth father as he did but different birth mothers. John Paul is very smart and took this news with understanding.

To show you how he took the news, he made a fist with his right hand and shot it up in the air and said "yea, I'm rich, I have more family than I can count. He was so happy and asked if he could meet the rest of his family sometime. There were tears all around and the most unspeakable joy in that group of people that they could hardly contain it.

Mary Ellen was a new person but with a whole heap of sorrow on her. Something she did have though, was forgiveness that gave her peace that passes all understanding in her soul. This is the peace that only God can give.

CHAPTER THIRTY-EIGHT

NEW ZEALAND

IN NEW ZEALAND, Mollie was doing very well physically and they were now planning their vacation to the United States come spring. John Paul was all excited because he had received pictures from his half brother and sister and he proudly showed them to all who would look at them He also sent a picture of him and his adoptive mom and dad to Max and Glory. They also exchanged pictures of Jimbo and Mister McDuffie. All the children felt so important to be sending and receiving mail from another country. Of course the adults were enjoying the pictures too. Everyone said John Paul looked just like Edward when he was that age.

In New Zealand, Margo said little Glory with her dark curly hair reminded her of someone but she didn't know who. She said I don't think I was old enough to remember what my mother looked like, but she kept going back and looking at the picture. She finally decided it must be that she looked a little like Starlita.

CHAPTER THIRTY-NINE

B Y THE TIME everyone got to Edwards and Juanita's house, Juanita had all the placement of bedrooms worked out. She had sleeping rooms for everyone. They had decided on Edwards place because it was the roomiest and would accommodate everyone. Mollie could not take the moving about so much so it was decided that they would all meet in one place and enjoy getting acquainted.

Juanita had cleaned and cooked and planned for so long. She felt honored that they would choose their place to stay. When they started to arrive, Edwards Mom and Dad had brought their motor home and parked it in their large, pretty yard. They had a hard time finding a place big enough to park it without ruining some of Juanita's flowers. She had every kind of blossom you can think of blooming everywhere. But they finally found a likely spot and parked it there. She would have to sleep fourteen adults and three children. That would be counting Starlita as one of the adults, as she was now just barely a teen but felt she was an adult.

John and Caroline Newburg would stay in their own room in the motor home. James and Lacey Cauldwell would stay in the motorhome too. Edward and Juanita would also be in the motor home much like when they went on vacation together. Russell and Mable O'Brian would have one suite in the guesthouse. And Adam and Martha Nielsen would have the other suite in the guesthouse. Mollie and Charley would have Edward and Juanita's room. Margo and Starlita would have Glory's room as it had twin beds in it and was close to the room Mollie would be in just in case she needed Margo in the night. Mary Ellen and Charles Wingate would have the guest en suite in the main house. It was decided that there were two sets of bunk beds left, one set in the motor home and one in the main house, Glory might be better to sleep in the motor home in one of the bunk beds since she was used to sleeping there and was used to her Mom and Dad sleeping there on vacation, and the two boys could sleep in the bunk beds in Max's room in the main house, as he would also be close to his adopted mom and dad who he was used to since everything would be strange to him.

They started coming in a few at a time until all were present. It was decided that they would all, after everyone was shown their rooms, meet in the big family room to introduce themselves. This would help John Paul get to know his new relatives and they could get to know him. As John Paul was introduced to each of his new grandparents, he walked up to each one and gave them a hug and whispered, "I know I'm going to love you". They were all astonished at his greeting and hugged him tight. Then he was introduced to his half- brother and half- sister. He said it's so strange that you have the same face, but I'm sure it's ok. I think we will be good friends as well as Half-brother and sister. Max and Glory said they were so glad to have another brother and would he like to go out and see their house? He was glad to do that as it was hard to sit still with the adults so long. All three children were glad to go. Max telling John Paul it was a club house and Glory telling him it was a play house. John Paul said well you could just call it "Club Playhouse". They all agreed that would work.

As they were talking, someone asked Margo how she had become acquainted with the Weston's. She said I was Married to Doctor Weston's brother. She told them the story of how they met. He was Starlita's father.

Margo said I will tell you about myself so you will know me better. You see, when I was very young, I was married to a nice man in Mexico and he was killed one night as he was coming home from work. I was pregnant with my first child. I had a really hard time after that for I was so young, just fifteen. I met another man who said he would help me get to the United States and we would be married. He told me I would have to leave my baby at the orphanage and he would come back as soon as we were settled and bring her to me. I believed him so I left her in the orphanage, but when we got to the United States he never went back to get her. He got real sick one day and died soon after. I tried to contact the orphanage when I got a little older and could think of what to do. I contacted the orphanage and they told me they don't have anyone there by that name. I think she must still be in Mexico and she must need me but I can find out nothing about her. I pray for my child every day, though she is not a child now. She looked at Juanita and said, "She has the same name as you." Juanita looked at Margo and said, "did you ever have any other name besides Margo that you went by?" Margo said why yes, I did. I changed my name from Margarita to Margo because it just seemed simpler for people to say. Juanita said and was your name ever Sanchez? Margo said yes, but how did you know? Then Juanita told her own story of how she was left in an orphanage as a baby and her mother never did come back to get her. She said for some reason, maybe from something she heard as a child, that she thought her mother had gone to the United States and that is why she was so anxious to get here to look for her mother. Edward has had a private detective looking for Margarita Sanchez but he could find no trace of her after a short time. Both Juanita and Margo stood at the same time and Margo said, my little girl, and at the same time Juanita said, my mother. They ran to each other's arms. Margo said, when she was able to talk, now I know why you look so much like my Starlita. She is your half-sister. Starlita shyly said, this is sure a time for half- sisters and half-brothers. That evening, they truly felt blessed. Tomorrow was Easter and they all were going to go to church where Juanita and Edward were married and were now members. The twins were used to going to Sunday school there too and invited John Paul to go with them.

CHAPTER FORTY

EASTER SUNDAY MORNING dawned bright and beautiful. After the children had gone to bed last night the ladies had colored eggs and fixed Easter baskets full of different kinds of candy. Starlita received a basket of sorts but it really turned into a purse and had some more grown up kind of candy in it along with a light lipstick and nail polish, a nail kit and some pretty clips for her hair. The kids were all excited but knew they didn't dive into these things until after church. They were all soon ready to go to church. The little guys in their new Easter suits and the girls in their new Easter dresses. The girls were even wearing new Easter hats. Caroline and Mable O'Brian had their new hats too, the ladies had spent quite a long time shopping and had a good time of it. They all looked quite festive, Charles Wingate told them.

When they got to church, there was quite a crowd but they did manage to get seated close to each other. When the pastor gave the sermon, he explained about Jesus dying on the cross to pay the debt for our sin and then how he rose again to a new life just as we do when we except him into our hearts, there was a quietness over the whole congregation as the choir sang joyously "HE AROSE TRIUMPHANTLY" Charles looked at Mary Ellen and saw tears running down her cheeks. He reached over and took her hand in his to let her know of his love for her. When church was over, everyone went to their cars slowly as there were many to greet on the way.

CHAPTER FORTY-ONE

WHEN THEY GOT home, the Colored eggs had mysteriously disappeared. Mitch was there waiting for them to get home. They all were surprised to see him except Edward, but even Edward was surprised to see Grace there. His comment was, "oh didn't I tell you he was coming?" There was a time of picture taking and then the kids changed their clothes to something more desirable to roll around in the grass with Mr. McDuffy. Meanwhile, the ladies saw to getting the food ready. It was a cold dinner of ham, homemade bread of many different kinds as each woman wanted to make her specialty bread. Potato salad coleslaw. Fruit salad sliced tomatoes, an array of pickles and olives of all kinds and a huge chocolate cake, strawberry shortcake and three kinds of cookies. The men had put up in the backyard tables and chairs for everyone. Edward had asked Mitch if he would bring the rented tables and chairs in his truck.

What a nice surprise, said Juanita, when she saw Grace. Grace had been so busy with school they had hardly seen her. When she got close enough Maxwell took Gloria Grace's hand and held up her left hand for all to see her engagement ring.

It was a beautiful day with a delicious dinner and an egg hunt with the children after dinner, and now Maxwell's big surprise. Everyone wanted to know when the wedding was but they got no answer there. They said they weren't sure because Grace said her mother, now that they had retired had time to plan her daughter's wedding and she and Grace would have to have hours and hours of mother daughter time to plan it. Grace had agreed that she would have any kind of wedding her mother wanted as long as Maxwell agreed. They looked at Maxwell and he shrugged his shoulders and said "hey, it can be any kind of wedding held anywhere as long as I get the prize at the end of that long trip down the aisle to the alter.

Earlier, when Star found her Easter basket that turned out to be a purse with light lipstick in it. She looked at her mother for she had not been allowed to wear it before. Her mother smiled at her and said I think you are old enough now Star. Everyone was just relaxing and sitting around watching the three kids hunt eggs. They saw the three children go into the play-club-house. They remarked how well they played together. The door opened and the three of them came to the group of adults with serious looks on their faces. John Paul was the speaker. He stepped forward and said we have talked this matter over and we would like to inform you politely that we did enjoy the dinner and the Easter baskets and the egg hunt today. But we would like this to be the last time you do this for us. We are just too old for this sort of thing now. We do thank you though for all of it. Glory stepped up and said I have something to say too. I enjoyed this today but I think I will be old enough next year to get something like Star got this year. I hope you agree. All the adults were having to cough or hide behind a handkerchief the smile that was on all faces. Mitch saved the day however, when he stepped up and said Glory, I think you are absolutely correct in what you say and John Paul and Max, I think you have the right Idea too. But if I were you, I would be thinking that something like my own tackle box or some kind of fishing gear would be in order. Max said with a grin, Uncle Max I think you are right as rain in this. Edward said that this is something that he and the others involved would do some thinking about.

A group of nineteen friends and family intermingled in some way, had just spent a lovely day together. First of all, going to church together to worship God and then coming back here and spending some wonderful peaceful worry free time together. But now it was about to come to an end. Each would go to their own home, some in this country and some in others. This had been a time to remember. They knew it was coming to a close and it saddened them a little. But they had so many pictures and memories to take with them until they could do this again.

The O'Brians went back to Minnesota to attend to their dairy farm. The Wingate's, Charles and Mary Ellen went back to their home in England, The Nielsen's Adam and Martha along with Charley and Mollie, Margo and Starlita.

Went back to New Zealand to their sheep ranch. James and Lacey Cauldwell went back to their home in Indiana along with John and Caroline Newburg. Juanita looked at Edward and said it's so quiet here. Edward smiled and said, it's kind of nice though isn't it? She had to agree, but it had been so nice to find her mother and to see John Paul for the first time, and just think Edward, I have a little half-sister! In the weeks to come there was lots of correspondence back and forth. Plans for Gloria Grace and Maxwell's wedding and the most wonderful news, Charles and Mary Ellen were expecting a child. Mary Ellen was overjoyed that God was giving her a second chance to be a mother and she was going to try to raise that child up to know her awesome God.

Mary Ellen told them in her next correspondence that Charles was coming to the United States in a week or two on business. He would try to see them if time permitted or at least call while he was there, but was anxious to get back home to be sure Mary Ellen was taking care of herself. He was very sweet wanting her to sit down all the time she said and pampering her during this pregnancy. She said she would be lazy if she followed his direction all the time. Let me know when you hear from Charles and assure him I am just fine and doing all the right things that this baby will be healthy when he comes into this world. Love to you all

PART TWO

A MAN CALLED EARL

Indianapolis Indian

CHAPTER FORTY-TWO

T HE BIG WHITE church on the corner of Arora Ave. and Bates Street had wide steps which lead up to its welcoming front doors that would be open on Sunday to greet everyone, but was at this time on a Monday morning tightly closed The sanctuary was at the top of these stairs. The ground floor level was where Pastor Carl Downey sat in his office looking out the window watching the tall man who had been walking past the church five times now. Pastor Carl asked God to show him how to help this man for he surely seemed to be lost or in need of some kind of help. He was wearing an expensive looking suit, but was a little rumpled looking as if he had been in the same clothes for some time. Pastor Carl decided he would go out and greet the man and ask if he could be of any help to him. Maybe the man was just lost. Indianapolis was not an easy town to find your way in unless you had lived there for a while. Why, he even got lost himself the other day while looking for the home of some new people who had visited the church and had asked for a visit when they filled out their visitor's card. They were looking for a church home in their new community.

As Pastor Carl walked up to him, he held out his hand and introduced himself and asked if he could help him in any way. The man did not give his name when Pastor Carl gave his, which seemed unusual but he didn't want to press him. I'm not sure, the man said, but I think I'm lost but I felt drawn to this church. What is your name sir? Pastor Carl asked. The man answered, Earl Merrell. He didn't know how he came up with that name, but maybe it is my name, he thought The Earl sounded right and the last name of Merrell was somehow familiar but something was wrong with it. It just didn't go together right somehow, but he had to come up with something quickly when the man asked for his name so he would just use this for now until he could figure this all out. Can I help you in any way Mister Merrell? Pastor Carl asked. Well I thought there was a hotel around here somewhere, he said. Pastor answered him, you are just a little off, for there is a big hotel just two blocks over to the west and two more blocks to the north. I think that might be the one you are looking for. Thanks a lot the man said, as he turned, held up his hand in a show of thanks and started off down the street. Pastor Carl prayed for the man as he went back inside, for he felt the man had a much bigger problem to face than just finding that hotel.

Well, for now at least, I have a name and that is a start even if it turns out to be wrong, Said Earl It's just that something seems wrong about it but yet something seems right. I'll just have to think about it some. He went in the direction of the hotel and came within sight of the huge building which was the hotel. He slowed his walk for he knew he could not go into the hotel without money or a credit card and he had neither. As he was nearing the hotel, a long vehicle drew up to the curb. Wow, what a limousine. This is not the hotel for me. A driver got out of the limousine and walked around the front to open the door for his passenger. A man got out of the rear of the limo and started around the front, waving to someone he was meeting across the street. As the driver was about to close the back door, a little girl jumped out of the car and ran after her Dad, calling to him to wait for her. The Dad didn't notice the little girl had stepped out of the limo and was starting to follow him. The driver, who was supposed to take her on to her preschool, tried to catch her but she slipped right passed him. There was a car coming fast and as Earl watched this, he knew the car was going to hit the little girl and so he ran as fast as he could and grabbed the child and pushed her out of the way, but he couldn't get out of the way soon enough to save himself and was hit by the oncoming vehicle. All was black as he went down.

CHAPTER FORTY-THREE

EARL WOKE UP in an unfamiliar place and was trying to get his bearings as a nurse walked in. He knew he must be in the hospital for this was certainly not the hotel. It had the smell of a hospital with all the disinfectant stuff they use. Then he remembered the child and the accident and asked about the child. He said did the child get hit? The nurse knew all about it for it made the news. She said the little girl was fine and he was quite the hero around here. She also said that someone wished to talk to him as soon as he was able. Also, she told him, she would have someone come in now and take his name and address for their records. He interrupted her to say, if I can leave soon I would like to go for I have no insurance and cannot pay. She told him her name was Irene and she had to get his name and address but he was not to worry about the bills. They were all being taken care of. He asked her who was taking care of the bills and she told him it was the father of the child he had saved. And now you must quit worrying and rest a little, because the doctor will be in soon and will discuss your injuries with you.

He lay there trying to remember. He knew the name, Earl Merrell, was not his real name exactly but it had to be something like that so he would use that for now and he must come up with some kind of address. He tried to remember where he had been, but it seemed useless as he could not even remember how he got to Indianapolis.

As he was trying to remember places that he had been, names of towns came to mind, but he didn't know if he had been there or remembered them from reading them on a map. Any one place would do, he thought. He would just pick one. At this point and time, one was as good as another. He thought he remembered going through a town somewhere near the border of Ohio, Indiana, named Harrington or something like that. All little towns had a State Street or an Elm Street didn't they? So he would just make up an address and he would ask that they try to keep it out of the papers as it might distress his aunt if she heard about it. He was getting good at this make-believe stuff and he was not proud of it. It didn't seem right but for now he would have to go with what seemed best.

He finally chose Earl Merrell, living at 19283East Elm Street, Harrington, Indiana. Before doing this though, he found himself fervently asking God to guide him in what he was doing. He asked forgiveness if it was wrong but he just didn't know what to do, so he was turning it over to Him.

Well, this was something new to learn about himself He must be a Christian and a praying one at that. It seemed natural to him to pray to God. That must be why he was so drawn to that church when he saw it.

When he was lying there thinking through all these things, the door opened and the nurse and a doctor came in, the doctor held out his hand and said I'm Doctor Hathaway, and what can I call you? My name is Earl Merrell and you can call me Earl and tell me I can go home now.

The doctor smiled and said not so fast now. You're our number one hero in this hospital so we are going to keep you for a little while. You do remember the accident, don't you? Earl said yes. I saw that child running and I knew she was going to get hit so I had just one thought in mind and that was to get to her as fast as I could to get her out of the way.

Well, you certainly did that, but you took quite a hit yourself. You have two broken legs and some internal injuries. I think everything is going to be alright though, except you won't be skiing or riding the waves on a surfboard for a while if you had any plans like that. No plans like that Doctor, Earl told him. Then you do what your good nurse here tells you and after a round or two of physical therapy to get those legs back in order, you will be good as new. Now I'll leave you with Nurse Irene. Earl looked at his nurse and saw what a beautiful woman she was. She had a head of the reddest hair he had ever seen. It wasn't exactly red but more rust color, but in a pretty way. She had a few freckles scattered over her nose and the biggest dark blue eyes he had ever seen. She was a real beauty and as he watched her move with such efficiency and grace around the room, he thought this was someone he could fall for. He immediately caught himself up realizing he didn't know if he had a wife already or not. He could not let himself get caught up in things like that now.

CHAPTER FORTY-FOUR

THE CHILD HE had saved was the daughter of the owner and CEO of one of the biggest restaurant chains around. His name was Frank Grandamere, owner of the Homestead House restaurants. He was working at having one in every state and was getting close. He was a very rich man and his little daughter Haylee was his pride and joy. She had just had her fifth birthday, and since her mother died, Haylee was his first priority.

Frank was wanting to meet this brave man who had taken the hit of that car to save his little Haylee. He loved his little daughter so much. She had the same rich dark brown hair that her mother had except Haylee's was curlier than her mothers'. She also had those deep brown eyes that Juliet, his wife had. He felt so lost when Juliet died but taking care of Haylee was what kept him going. He had to make it right with this man. He got the go ahead, to speak to the gentleman this afternoon and he wanted to be there at two, when his Doctor visit was over for the day so he could get to know him, and find out how he could help him. He had already been praying for him and had his prayer group at church praying too. At two o'clock, he knocked on the door of room twenty-three and no one responded. He looked around and saw a nurse coming toward him. She spoke and said her name was Irene and she bet he was looking for the hero of this floor, and smiled as she said Earl Merrell. He said yes that was who he was looking for and was told he could talk with him as soon as he was back from X-Ray. Nurse Irene told him they were running a little late but he would be here soon. She showed him into a little sitting room just down the hall, with some comfortable chairs and told him she would bring Earl there as soon as he got back. Frank used this time while he was waiting to ask God to guide him on how he could help this man. When Earl came in he was in a wheel chair but looking cheerful, for all he had been through.

Frank introduced himself and shook hands with Earl and was thanking him so much that Earl had to stop him. Frank asked if there was someone he could fly out here to stay with him while he was recuperating. Earl was anticipating these questions and had made up his story. Earl said he was alone in the world except for a great aunt, but didn't know where she was now as they hadn't kept in touch. Frank felt so sorry for Earl and really wanted to do something for him.

CHAPTER FORTY-FIVE

IN TALKING TO Earl, Frank Grandamere couldn't find out too much about him. He seemed to be a man of few words, a very private person and Frank would respect that. He did find out that Earl had no relatives in the area or even acquaintances for that matter. The man seemed so alone in the world. Frank was determined he would do all he could to help this man. Earl told him he was here seeking a better job. When asked what he was looking for, ledgers seemed to be in his mind and he said he was a book keeper. He sure hoped he had some kind of background to substantiate that. It just seemed right to him. He could almost see the ledgers in his mind. He wished he could see a name as well.

Frank told Earl he was not to worry about the hospital bill and when he was able to work, he had a job waiting for him. This was a great relief to Earl. This at least took care of his immediate problems. Nurse Irene talked to Earl daily and they became good friends. Irene thought Earl was someone she could fall in love with. She loved his gentle ways and the way he interacted with Haylee who came to see him every day. Haylee loved to play games with Earl and would always try to get Irene to play with them. When Earl asked her what her last name was, she told him it was Kirk. She liked the way he softly said Irene Kirk, a pretty name for a pretty lady. It seemed Haylee was falling for Irene Kirk too. One day, when she was tired, she asked Irene if she would read her a story like her mom used to do. Irene knew she was getting too attached to the child, but could not refuse her anything.

CHAPTER FORTY-SIX

IN TIME THE casts were taken off of Earl's legs and then the painful but needed physical therapy started. Physical therapy was helping Earl to walk so much better, he was looking forward to getting out of the hospital soon, but where would he go? He hadn't figured that out yet. When Frank Grandamere came in one day walking down the hall whistling a tune and seeming very happy about something. He had come without Haylee that day which was a bit unusual. He saw Earl and said, hey there Earl old chum. I hear you are going to get busted out of this place soon, and I have some news for you. I have a job for you if you are willing to take it and it comes with living quarters and best of all, it is in my office building where you will be working, so no travel time or expense getting to work. Now how is that for a win, win situation? Sounds good on my end but how do you know I will be able to do the job you want done? Well, Frank said, my accountant, who just got engaged, will be moving out of the rooms that come with the job, for he plans to move away after he is married. He gave his notice but will stay on until you are familiar with the job and are comfortable with it. That sounds great, said Earl, as he marveled at how things were working out for him. He knew it had to be God at work.

The next day which was a Saturday was moving day. Earl would be moving into his apartment. It was furnished already and when they got there Earl saw that there was a brand new easy lounge chair with the tags still on it. He was going to have to have help for a while and somehow Frank had pulled some strings and got Irene as his nurse as long as she was needed. Earl was introduced to Larry Moore who was the previous accountant and would be showing Earl his method of keeping the books. It was all very familiar to Earl. He knew he would have no problem with this job. He just wished he knew what books he took care of before. It might give him a clue as to who he was and where he came from. He kept feeling that someone was waiting for him to return. Some folks remarked that he spoke with an English accent, but he couldn't remember anything about England.

Earl was settling into a routine of working in the morning until time for Irene to come and the therapist would give him his workout and then Irene would fix his dinner. About this time he would have company in the form of a vivacious little dark haired girl named Haylee, who Earl was sure came more to see Irene than to see him. He loved watching them together. He knew it reminded him of some phase of his life but he just couldn't get it worked out. Before she would leave, Haylee would insist that Irene read her a bedtime story even thought it was too early for bedtime and Haylee was just leaving to go to her own home.

CHAPTER FORTY-SEVEN

I T WAS JUST a matter of time before Earl noticed a spark between Irene and Frank. He was so happy for them for he knew Irene was longing for a home and a family of her own and he truly could tell she already loved that little motherless child as much as that child loved her.

Frank asked Irene to go to dinner with him one evening and she accepted. It was the start of a beautiful romance between the three, for Haylee at once put herself right in the middle of it. He also asked her to help with Haylee's birthday party, and in doing so, she met the rest of his friends for it was a big party that included adults of all the children. Most of his friends she had met at church, but there were some that were known through his business. It soon became clear to everyone that they were meant for each other. One evening they went out for a special dinner and when they came back, Irene was wearing a big shiny ring on the ring finger of her left hand and was quick to show everyone. When asked, when is the big day? Haylee spoke up and said, we don't know yet but it will be soon for

I am going to be flower girl because that is always the job of the child. I saw that in a book once. Haylee thought of something else and said. I don't think anyone is going to give Daddy away, just someone will give Irene to us. And we will be a full family again. That is how it goes isn't it Dad? Something like that, Frank told her. Everyone tried to hide their smiles as they watched how seriously Haylee was taking it all.

Earl, after moving into his new quarters and taking on his new job, was beginning to think this was all going to work out. He still knew there was something missing in his life but he didn't know what to do about it, so he just worked his job and saved all the money he could because he felt he needed to even though he was well paid and felt his job was pretty secure. He had built up a sizeable bank account and with all that was taking place such as the wedding, no one noticed how quiet he was, and how he never got very involved in anything.

He went to church every Sunday with the family and constantly prayed to God to help him find his way back home, for he felt he had a home and maybe even a family somewhere.

CHAPTER FORTY-EIGHT

IN ENGLAND, MARY Ellen was beginning to worry about Charles. He had been gone a long time without a word from him. He hadn't been feeling well when he left England to fly to America to meet with his business partner there. He said it might take a little more time than he wanted to be away, but he would be in touch with her, and would be back as soon as possible. Her pregnancy was going along well but now it was getting closer to her time, and she was really worrying now. When she called her father and stepmother to see if he had called them, she was really worried when they said they hadn't heard a word from him. She knew he wanted to be with her when the baby came. She had written to the Newburg's in Indiana to tell them that Charles would be contacting them while he was there. She had not had a word from then either. She decided she would wait until this Sunday and if she had not heard from anyone by then, she would call Juanita and Edward. She knew they usually went to church, but came home to have family day in the afternoon.

When she placed her call Sunday afternoon to the Newburg's, it was with prayer to God that they would know something or have some word from Charles. Edward answered the phone and when he heard who it was he called Juanita to pick up the phone so they could both talk. Juanita asked her how her pregnancy was going and she told her but as soon as she could break into their excited talking she asked them when they had last heard from Charles. They said they had received her letter saying he would call but they were still waiting to hear from him. This was what she had feared she would hear for she knew he would have called her by now if he could. When she explained to them, they were so worried about her. She had Charles dad there with in telephone reach, but she needed someone else there. Edward said he would call his mother and he knew she would want to be there with her. He also told her they would pray and have their church pray for her and for Charles safety. He hung up but Juanita kept talking to her. Edward picked up his cell phone and called his mother and told her all that was going on. Caroline Newburg was ready to go to help her deceased friend's, only daughter, for she had been friends with Mary Ellen's mother, Pearl Cauldwell for a long time. She told Edward to get her a flight on the first plane out and call her back and she would be ready to go. Edward was able to get her a flight that would leave that night. She would have a short layover in New York, but would arrive in England tomorrow morning. Juanita was still on the phone and relayed all the information to Mary Ellen. It was such a relief for Mary Ellen she just sank down on her couch and thanked God for answers to the prayers of Gods people, Mary Ellen drifted off into a peaceful sleep and was still sleeping when Caroline Newburg knocked on her door the next day at almost noon.

Caroline didn't try to call someone to pick her up. She thought it would be better if she just got a taxi to take her, and she knew she had made the right choice when she got to the house and found that Mary Ellen had been able to nap while she waited for her to get there. Mary Ellen had not had much sleep for a while and she really needed the rest. They talked for a while and Caroline tried to get Mary Ellen to eat something for the sake of the baby. She was due any time now and Caroline was so worried for her. It had been a long time since anyone had heard from Charles and they both knew that something had happened to Charles or he would have been in touch with them. He had been so happy about this baby and had been reluctant to go on the business trip at all, but Mary Ellen had assured him she was fine and he would be back in plenty of time to be with her when the baby came. Now she knew she was going to have this baby without him. She had to truly trust in God to help her through this time of trouble. Caroline wanted to read a scripture to Mary Ellen, so she had Mary Ellen rest on the couch. As she opened her Bible, She asked Mary Ellen to close her eyes and just listen to some of Gods promises.

She read Jeramiah 29 11 to her. "For I know the plan I have for you, declares the Lord. Plans to prosper you and not to harm you. Plans to give you hope and a future." You see Mary Ellen, God is still in control of this whole situation. We can't understand it now and we don't know where Charles is. But we do know that God knows where he is right this minute and we just have to trust Him. Caroline then turned to Psalms 23 and read to her. "The Lord is my Shepherd". Remember when you were in New Zealand and how the Shepherds cared so well for their sheep? God is our tender caring shepherd now. Then she continued reading, "I shall not want. He makes me lay down in green pastures" Mary Ellen remember those beautiful green rolling pastures in New Zealand? She continued reading, "He restores my soul Yea though I walk through the valley of the shadow of death, I will fear no evil". Mary Ellen we know that God is not letting Charles experience evil because He is there with him. And where the Bible says I will fear no evil for Thou art with me "God is with you the same as He is with Charles. "My rod and my staff will comfort you." Charles as well as you will both be comforted by your Heavenly Father. She continued reading softly to the end of Psalms 23 "Thou prepares a table before me in the presence of my enemies. My cup runneth over, surely goodness and mercy will follow me all the days of my life and I will dwell in the house of the Lord forever." So you see Mary Ellen, we just have to trust in the lord that He will make it all clear to us when it is time.

Mary Ellen looked up at Caroline and smiled. She was so thankful to God for sending Caroline to be with her since her own mother was gone. How she missed her now and wished she would have had a better relationship with her mother while she was still on this earth. She was going to trust God to help her bring this baby into the world and if God did not see fit to bring Charles back to them, she would raise this child to know God and to trust Him in all things.

CHAPTER FORTY-NINE

EARL WAS STILL trying to figure out what he should be doing to find out who he was. He lost sleep at night just thinking and trying to remember. Sometimes something would almost be there in his mind and before he could get it clear, it would be gone. He worried that he had a family somewhere that was waiting for him to come home and at these times he would cry out to God to take care of them until he could get to them. He dreamed once that he had a child and when he woke up, he didn't know if it was a boy or girl and no name would come to him.

He just kept doing his job and going to church. Some of his friends at church would try to do match making and get him involved with a girl but he would tell them he was a bachelor and would shy away from any involvement with a woman. He just couldn't take the chance in case he had someone waiting for him.

Just about everyone he had met and knew since he had first seen the big white church now went to that church as did he. He thought of this time as his starting point. That is where he woke up to realize he didn't know who he was or where he was and how he had come to be there. He had kept his secret from all of them and he didn't know why. Maybe he was some kind of criminal or something. He didn't think so but how could he be sure? He knew he didn't have any feelings like that now. He would just go on the way he was until God changed something in his life.

The church and Pastor Carl Downey was planning a homecoming and Pastor Carl had asked Charles to help him with it. Charles said he had never done anything like that but would be glad to do whatever he could if they just tell him how. He had never heard of a church having a home coming, but Pastor Carl explained to him that the church was going to experience a birthday. It was one hundred years old this year. Not that particular building but from the time the church was first started in someone's living room. Soon it grew and they rented a storefront building and as God blessed they built their own little church and as soon as they outgrew that they built another. It was the history of the church. In this length of time many people had moved away and others had come. This was an effort to get an invitation out to all the members who had at one time come to this church and they would all meet and have a potluck dinner at the church. Members living close would furnish all of the side dishes and the church would furnish the meat. Members who had moved away could just bring bread or whatever was convenient for them. Many of the folks hadn't seen each other in a long time so it would be a wonderful time of renewing friendships. Pastor Carl kept Earl busy looking up different ones and getting the invitations out. Some were close and some as far away as New Zealand.

When John and Caroline Newburg got their invitation, Caroline was in England with Mary Ellen. She had her baby with no trouble but was so despondent that Caroline would not leave. Mary Ellen would only brighten up when she was holding her baby girl. She refused to put a name on the birth certificate until she could discuss it with Charles. She was sure Charles would come home someday. So the baby's name was listed as baby girl and that is what they called her. Caroline hoped that in time she would realize that Charles was forever lost to them but Mary Ellen would not hear of it.

When John got the invitation, he called his wife and said he thought it would be a good thing for her to bring Mary Ellen and the baby back home to the rest of the family. When Caroline mentioned this to Mary Ellen, she was excited to go if the doctor said the baby could travel without problems. The Doctor assured her the baby would be fine and thought it would be good for Mary Ellen too. So now they had plenty to keep them busy getting ready to go. Soon tickets were purchased and all was ready. John would meet their flight.

Edward and Juanita and the twins, Glory and Max were going to the homecoming too. Of course everyone was wanting to see Mary Ellen and Charles' new Baby. Margarita Sanchez received her invitation in New Zealand and planned to go to see her daughter Juanita and her family. So many had at one time or another been at that church and had moved on but now would meet there again and renew old acquaintances. Edward's friends, Michal Denton, who used to be co-owner of the cabin in the woods until Edward had bought him out and made it into the Mansion for his family. Edward's cousin, Grace Lynn and Maxwell Mitchell. Edwards's twins, Glory and Max were named after these two friends. They were married now, having met at Edwards and Juanita's, and fell deeply in love. It was certainly going to be quite a homecoming for a number of people. Mary Ellen was just hoping to somehow find some trace of her husband, Charles.

CHAPTER FIFTY

THE DAY OF the Homecoming dawned bright and sunshiny. It looked like it was going to be a beautiful day for the occasion. The kitchens in many homes were already sending out such mouthwatering aromas.

Mary Ellen was in her room with her daughter, talking to God about Charles and asking for God to somehow increase her faith. She was remembering the passage she had learned as a child in Sunday school that if we had faith as big as a grain of mustard seed we could move mountains. She remembered how her teacher had showed them a mustard seed. It was so small. She didn't think she had ever seen anything that small. Lord I do trust and believe in you as much as I can. Now will you help what I am lacking in belief? I believe you led me to this place today even though I know everyone else thinks it is just false hope that I have. I don't know why you have allowed Charles to be gone so long and under these circumstances, but you must have a reason. Help me to learn from this and please restore Charles to me. In your son's name this daughter is asking this. When Mary

Ellen came out of her room, she had a peace in her heart that passes all understanding.

The church was full and the smells coming from the kitchen was delightful. Earl had been in his apartment which was right down the block and around the corner from the church. When he left his apartment to walk to the church, the nearer he got to the church he could smell the good smells from the church kitchen. Before he left his apartment, he had been talking to God saying that he so wanted to find out who he was and quit living this lie. He had begun to think of what he was doing as a lie. He just didn't know how else to handle it. He prayed that if anyone was here that could shed any light on his situation, they would make it known to him somehow. He did so want a family and had such a strong feeling he had one somewhere.

As he neared the church, he was nearing the crowd of people who had spilled out onto the grounds of the church, he almost went back for he was very nervous. He calmed himself though and began to enjoy talking to people he knew. He suddenly felt a great need to unburden himself to someone. He had talked to God so long this morning and thought he had everything under control. Now though, he felt completely undone and knew he needed to talk to Pastor Carl. He saw him coming toward him and asked if he could talk to him. Pastor Carl said sure, what's up? Earl said no, I mean could I talk to you in private. Pastor looked at him and recognized there was a problem. He put all other duties aside in his mind and brought Earl into his office and shut the door.

Pastor Carl realized there was something so heavy on this man's mind, so he asked if Earl would mind if he prayed first. Earl said please do. Pastor Carl simply asked God to take charge of this meeting and work it out in His wonderful way and if a miracle was needed, please supply it at just the right time. Pastor Carl didn't know why he prayed as he did for he had no idea a miracle of any kind was needed. After the prayer, he looked at Earl and when Earl opened his mouth, the first thing he said was I don't think my real name is Earl.

CHAPTER FIFTY-ONE

WHEN EARL OPENED his mouth and said he thought his name was not really Earl, he just couldn't stop. He started telling about when he was first drawn to the church and realized he didn't have a clue as to who he was and how he had got there. As he talked, the whole story came out.

Pastor Carl was sure he had never had so strange and delicate a problem brought to him before. A different man might have said "why me Lord?" But not this man. Pastor Carl, after listening to Earl's whole story, told him they would work on this together with the help of the Lord. He said, the only thing to do was to go to God again, telling him they were giving this burden to Him to deal with because they had a homecoming to take care of. He told Earl to stay close to him and they would see what God was going to make of this. Pastor reminded Earl that God said all things work together for good for them who love the Lord and are the called according to His purpose. I believe God is going to make this day one to remember for all of us. Just remember as we open this door, and go out to join the others, God is at work and is still in complete control. Trusting God to lead them, they opened the door and walked out to blend in with the rest of the people.

Earl saw a man coming toward him with a huge smile on his face. Earl whispered a prayer to God saying this is it Lord, for I don't know this man coming with outstretched hand to meet me but I think he knows me. Help me now.

It was Maxwell Mitchell. He said in his booming voice, Charles, my friend, good to see you. How is your sweet wife Mary Ellen, and did she have that baby yet? Juanita has kept us up to date but it's been a while since we heard from her. Earl heard all this and was trying to process it all but knew he was losing the battle. As everyone within hearing distance looked, the blood ran from Earl's face as he slowly crumpled to the floor.

CHAPTER FIFTY-TWO

PASTOR CARL KNEW what had happened. Someone from Earls past was there and had recognized him. The shock of hearing his wife's name and that they were expecting a child was just too much for him to take in. This was something Earl was not sure about and had him worried as he talked to Pastor earlier. As he stayed unconscious, someone called for an ambulance to take him to the hospital.

It was just at this time that Mary Ellen and the baby were arriving with Edward and Juanita Newburg. They did not see who was taken away in the ambulance so they just continued to get out of the car taking out a lot of things they thought they would need for the baby for the day. Pastor Carl took a microphone that had been used earlier in the singing session they had, and asked for everyone's attention. He got complete silence as all wanted to know what had just happened. He asked for the Newburg's and all that came with them to please go to his office. He was able to open a door from his office to one of the Sunday school rooms to make his office larger when needed for just such a time as this. Although this was just the second time he had used it, he was surely glad today, they had fixed it so he could make use of it. He had called a few more people in who he knew would be concerned about Earl. He had asked their minister of music to tell the people he would give them reports about the man taken to the hospital as soon as news came in. He asked all of them to bow their heads and pray for the man, reminding them that where two or three are gathered God would be with them. After the fervent prayer, he asked that all leaders please take charge of their children of the age they were assigned to get their games started. The rest would have a song fest as the men set up tables and the ladies got the food ready. He went into his office again and closed the door.

Then John and Caroline Newburg, James and Lacey Cauldwell, Mary Ellen and the baby all had just entered when they heard this announcement. They were puzzled but asked someone to show them to the office. There were a few others going too. His opening statement to everyone was, I want to tell you the story of a man named Earl.

CHAPTER FIFTY-THREE

S OME OF YOU know him by the name of Earl. Some of you know him by the name of Charles. Actually, he is both. Now while we wait to hear from the doctor who is with him now, I want to ask you to do this. Try to imagine waking up to the knowledge that you are walking down a street in a strange town and you don't know your name or how you got there and can find not even a scrap of paper to help you. This is what happened to this man called Earl. Mary Ellen knew they had found her Charles and could hardly sit there, but Caroline and Mary Ellen's dad were on each side of her and when she whispered to them that she must go to him, her dad put his arm around her and told her Charles was in good hands and now they must listen to find out what had happened to Charles and for now, just put him in God's hands. Now the doctor who has been with him is here and would like to talk to you. Doctor Nelson go ahead. As Doctor Nelson talked, he explained at once that the patient was not in any medical danger and was healthy except for his memory loss and the stress that had caused.

Even now though he is starting to remember things. This causes him worry and stress so we are keeping him sedated much of the time so he can handle the stress and process a little at a time what he remembers. We do not know what causes something like this to happen, but we do know that the good news is that in almost all cases such as this one, he will most likely start to remember and eventually have a complete recovery of his memory loss.

Now I will turn this meeting back over to your pastor who will tell you the rest of the story and by visiting hours tonight you will be able to see him. We ask you to limit it to relatives only for a few days. Let this man get his bearings again. When Pastor Carl took the mike, he said now as soon as I have thanked the Lord for His goodness in all this, I will tell you the rest of the story of this man called Earl. Everyone bowed his head as Pastor offered a prayer of thanksgiving to his merciful God.

He then related to them how he had first seen the man walking past the church and realized he was lost or had some kind of problem. Then how the man had become the hero by saving the little girl, Haylee Grandamere. He was the hero but was taken to the hospital with two broken legs where he stayed through the mending of the legs and all the physical therapy that went with it. He was relieved to know that his bills were all being paid by Haylee's father, but he had to give a name and address so he tried to think and Earl came up in his mind and he grabbed at that name thinking, maybe that is my name. He actually is the Earl of Wyngate. Then he had to come up with a last name and all he could come up with was Merrell. He knew it wasn't just right but it was close to something in his life. We know now he was trying to get Mary Ellen's name and the closest he could come was Merrell. This thinking process is the way the mind works. At the mention of this Mary Ellen, who was seated for her legs would not hold her up, started to cry, she said he was thinking of me all along. Pastor Carl continued, he made up the address and when asked about a job he knew there was some sort of ledgers in his past so he said he was an accountant and was hired immediately by Grandamere and given a place to live. I want all of you to remember how you prayed for this man when you found out he was missing and now, think how God was answering your prayer all along. When the homecoming plans were made, Earl told me the whole story.

He was afraid someone might know him and also that no one would know him and he would not ever find out who he really was. It was a very stressful time for him. He told me he was so afraid he had a family somewhere that was suffering somehow by his absence. He just wanted to find out about them. Also he was beginning to dream about holding a little baby but couldn't come up with a name or who that baby belonged to. He said there was also the thought that maybe he had committed a crime but he didn't think so. All these thoughts were constantly going through his mind. So when you are allowed to see him, before you open that door, ask God to guide you in what you say and how you say it so as not to cause this man called Earl, any more stress but just Gods love. I know you all want this for him.

A few weeks later, when Charles finally did get enough of his memory back and had met most of his relatives, he couldn't get enough of looking at Mary Ellen and his wonderful little girl. When he found out she didn't have a name yet, he wanted to remedy that right away. Charles and Mary Ellen talked about this for hours and decided to name this precious one, Mary Pearl after her mother and her grandmother. So Mary Pearl Wyngate it was.

EPILOGUE

AFTER LONG VISITS with both old friends and new ones they had made, Charles had finally been released from his doctor to travel, they headed for England and Wyngate Manor. Things also settled down in Ednita Mansion and all things were getting back to normal at the Church, after such a memorable home coming.